'Are you Sidney

'Yes?'

She was even prettier than her photograph, Shayne realized. With hair like a golden sunset and skin the colour of honey.

What was she doing here in Alaska?

'I'm Shayne Kerrigan. Ben's brother.'

'Why isn't Ben here?'

Because he's a coward, Shayne wanted to say. *Grown men didn't propose to one woman, and marry another.*

He stared at Sydney. 'Look, there's no easy way to tell you. Ben's old fiancée showed up, and they're getting married. Might already be married.'

Shayne faltered when he saw the look of distress enter her eyes. He saw the struggle she was waging not to cry. Admiration whispered through him.

'Why don't I buy you a plane ticket—'

'No. I came to start a new life and that's what I'm going to do.'

He refused to think over what he was about to say. 'All right, you can stay with me.'

Dear Reader,

Seasons greetings from Silhouette Special Edition®. We are pleased to present you with some real gifts in this month's festive line-up.

Perennial favourite Cathy Gillen Thacker has come up with a real Christmas cracker—find out if mother-to-be Kate Montgomery and Dr Michael Sloane, the father of her unborn child, settle their differences in time for *Baby's First Christmas*. And a mail-order mix-up leaves the *wrong* brother marrying the *right* bride in Marie Ferrarella's *Wife in the Mail*.

Sexy sheriff Justin Adams breaks all his own rules by helping desperate single mother Patsy Langhorn in Sherryl Woods's *Natural Born Lawman*. And Joe McConnell wants to change all the rules when he discovers a son he never knew he had. Could he ask his wife to be a mother to his child? Don't miss *Unexpected Family* from Laurie Campbell.

College sweethearts meet up again, and Brent Morrison is about to discover *why* Blythe ran out on him all those years ago in Jackie Merritt's *The Secret Daughter*, the last part of THE BENNING LEGACY trilogy.

Finally, a passionate encounter and Caitlin's in trouble—the 6lb 12oz kind!—that's Lois Faye Dyer's *The Only Cowboy for Caitlin*.

Happy Christmas reading, and come back to us in 2000!

The Editors

MARIE FERRARELLA
Wife in the Mail

SILHOUETTE
SPECIAL EDITION®

Silhouette, Silhouette Special Edition and Colophon are registered trademarks of Harlequin Books S.A., used under licence.

First published in Great Britain 1999
Silhouette Books, Eton House, 18-24 Paradise Road,
Richmond, Surrey TW9 1SR

© Marie Rydzynski-Ferrarella 1998

ISBN 0 373 24217 4

23-9912

Printed and bound in Spain
by Litografia Rosés S.A., Barcelona

To
Dorothy Provine Day,
who first made me aware of Alaska
and gave me a goal to aspire to.
Thank you.

MARIE FERRARELLA

lives in southern California. She describes herself as the tired mother of two over-energetic children and the contented wife of one wonderful man. This Romance Writers of America RITA award-winning author is thrilled to be following her dream of writing full-time.

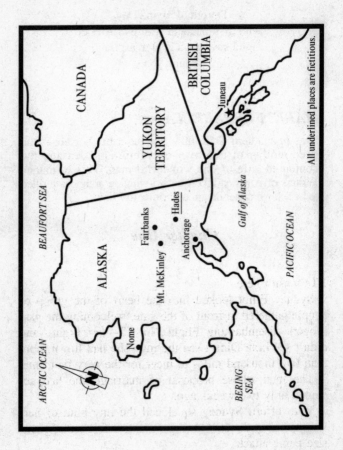

All underlined places are fictitious.

Chapter One

He wasn't here.

Sydney Elliot looked into the heart of the group of people gathered in front of the gate, welcoming the passengers disembarking Flight No. 17—*her* flight—and didn't see him. Didn't see the man she had flown more than two thousand miles to meet for the very first time.

The man whose proposal of marriage she had accepted only two weeks ago.

With effort, Sydney squelched the tiny bout of nervousness that threatened to grow into a full-scale, giant-size panic attack.

It was all right. He'd come. He'd promised he would be here and he would be. Time was just a relative thing; wasn't that something he'd written to her? That time up here in Alaska didn't mean the same thing it did in the other forty-nine states? It moved slower, more languidly, like a fish sunning itself in the stream after the first thaw.

All around Sydney people were being welcomed, hugged, kissed. Just in front of her, a woman was embraced by a huge, burly man while two children wiggled between them, eager to share in the homecoming, in the love that was so visibly there.

The scene warmed her. It was what she had come for. To find love again, or perhaps for the first time. To find a place for herself where she was needed.

What if he'd changed his mind?

What if he didn't come?

Trying to still the small, gnawing doubt within her that could, at any second, mushroom into something far less manageable, Sydney scanned the area, hoping to see a tall, broad-shouldered man hurrying through the doors in the rear of the terminal. Hurrying toward her.

There was no one like that.

Sydney shifted her carry-on luggage to her other hand. The strap was beginning to bite into her skin. There was no reason to panic. He'd obviously been delayed. After all, it wasn't as if he could just roll out his door to reach the airport. Ben Kerrigan lived some hundred miles away and, as he'd said in his last letter, at this time of year, even though it was fall, the road to Anchorage wouldn't be readily accessible by car. Ben had written that he'd have to fly his plane from Hades to get here.

Maybe he'd had to refuel first. Or maybe he'd gotten a late start. There were a hundred reasons why he wasn't here. She just had to pick one to focus on.

For a second Sydney shut her eyes to pull herself together. Panic wasn't her normal way of dealing with things. Ever since she was a little girl, she'd always been the levelheaded, practical one.

How levelheaded and practical had it been to uproot her entire life, pack it into a moving van and take off for the Alaskan terrain just because a man she had never met had asked her to marry him?

A smile curved her mouth as she recalled her best friend Marta's exact words on the subject. "Are you out of your mind?"

But she wasn't out of her mind, Sydney assured herself. She'd never been more serious, never been more sure of anything in her life than when she'd handed in her resignation to the principal of the elementary school where she taught, terminated her lease, sold most of her furniture and contracted Over The Hill Movers to move the most precious of her possessions not just over the hill, but halfway across the country.

Funny how fate managed to manipulate things. If she hadn't been in her dentist's office and picked up the magazine with the article about Alaska in it, she wouldn't be here. Ben had written the article and she had been completely captivated by his vitality. When he'd said that waking up in Alaska was like being reborn each morning, she knew she'd found her answer, her chance to turn things around for herself. She'd wanted to thank him for opening her eyes, so she'd written him a letter in care of the magazine. Less than a month later, there was a letter from him. After that, there were many letters, and over the course of eight months her future was finally forged.

Something had come to life in Sydney each time she'd read Ben's letters over the past eight months. Letters filled with the wonder of the place where he lived. Letters that made each moment in life seem like an adventure—fresh, exciting and precious out here in this pristine world. They reminded her of the letters that her Aunt Faye used to send to her father. Aunt Faye had made her life in Alaska. There was that same enthusiasm coming through. Ben's letters had also revealed his uncanny sensitivity for her feelings. A sensitivity that, in her time of need, had reached out to her. It was as if this man, living so far away in his icy domain, understood her. More than that, he understood what she needed. To be part of something, to be necessary, and to be loved.

The words in his letters made her feel that she could be all three. There was no question in her mind as she'd accepted his proposal that Dr. Ben Kerrigan was her soul mate.

There was also no question that he was still not here.

Sydney sighed as she struggled to ignore the strange, discomfiting premonition of dread, of something being wrong, that whispered insistently across her mind.

It was just prenuptial jitters, with a dash of jet lag thrown in, nothing more. She had to get hold of herself or else, when he did arrive, he'd take one look at her, turn on his heel and flee.

The group around her thinned. Very soon, there were no more passengers disembarking Flight No. 17. Except for the attendant closing the doors behind her, Sydney stood alone.

The look in the woman's eyes when she turned around told Sydney that there would be no stragglers coming off her plane. It was empty.

As empty as Sydney suddenly felt.

A genial, sympathetic look crossed the attendant's face as she approached Sydney. "May I help you?" The gently asked question resounded of kindness itself.

Sydney almost asked her if she knew Dr. Ben Kerrigan, but there was no earthly reason why the young woman should. He didn't practice here. Anchorage was large by Alaskan standards. It was Hades that was small.

Everyone there knew who Ben Kerrigan was. The doctor who, along with his brother, ran the only medical clinic in a hundred-mile radius.

Sydney merely shook her head.

"My ride's been delayed," she murmured. Until he finally arrived and found her, she had to get her things together. She licked a very dry lower lip and looked at the woman inquisitively. "Your baggage claim area is...?" With a comforting hand on Sydney's shoulder, the flight attendant turned her around and pointed to a huge white arrow suspended from the ceiling. Its sole function was to indicate the location of the down escalator.

"To your right as you get off the escalator. You can't miss it," she promised.

Sydney wasn't all that sure about that. She had a tendency to get lost very easily, even when things were clearly marked. That was another reason Marta had thought her coming out here insane.

"Give it up, Sydney. Nobody's a mail-order bride anymore, for crying out loud. Think," she'd all but begged two nights ago as she'd watched her pack. "You're going off into the wilderness, Sydney. You know what you're like. You'll get lost in the first damn snowdrift that crosses your path."

Sydney had laughed at the woman she'd known ever since her senior year in college. She'd taken no offense at the anger in Marta's voice, knowing that Marta only had her best interest at heart.

"Snowdrifts don't cross your path, Marta," she'd said, closing her last suitcase firmly and flipping the locks. "They're stationary."

"They have more sense than you do, then," Marta had moodily declared.

Maybe they did at that, Sydney thought now.

A moot point; she was here. This was going to be her new home. A fresh start. It was what she needed, what she wanted.

She focused on that.

Feeling somewhat better, Sydney shouldered her purse, shifted her carry-on back to her right hand and made her way to the escalator.

It's going to be all right, Sydney promised herself soothingly. *Ben's just late. Happens all the time here. Probably.*

People marked time differently in Alaska, that was all, she told herself again. Life had a more basic, less complicated purpose here. Wasn't that what had drawn her to Alaska to begin with? That, and Ben's letters. Or, more to the point, the man she'd discovered within the letters. An exciting, charming, intelligent man who made her feel alive again. The fact that the photos he'd sent showed him to be extremely good-looking was a bonus that fate had seen fit to throw in. If he'd lived anywhere but here, Sydney knew that Ben would have had his pick of anyone he wanted. But women were scarce in Hades, Alaska. And Ben had picked her.

At least she wouldn't have to worry about him running off just before the wedding and breaking her heart the way Ken had, she thought.

Gingerly, balancing her carry-on in front of her, offsetting it with the weight of her large, crammed purse, she stepped onto the escalator. As the metal stairs rhythmically made their way into the ground floor, she scrutinized the area, looking for any sign of him.

Dr. Ben Kerrigan was everything she had ever wanted in a man. Sydney'd known that a month into their correspondence, known from the way he wrote about his life out here with the unbridled joy of a child discovering everything for the first time. That, coupled with his dedication to his work, had made him perfect in her eyes.

So he was a little late, so what? In the grand scheme of things, that didn't mean anything. He'd be here soon enough.

Sydney was positive that Ben Kerrigan wasn't the type of man to go back on a promise. She had willingly bet her soul on it.

What was he doing here, looking for some woman who shouldn't even have been on the plane? If she'd had a single spark of sense in her head, this woman would have changed her mind, turned in her airline ticket, and stayed put.

He'd arrived late, almost not coming to the airport at all. And he didn't want to be here, he wanted to be at his clinic, working. Or even at home, awkwardly wrestling with the new role of fatherhood into which he'd suddenly been thrown.

Being a doctor in Alaska was a full-time job. There was no time for anything else. Which was why Barbara had left Alaska in the first place he reminded himself. Because he'd given too much of himself to his practice and not enough to her. Now that his ex-wife was dead, where the hell was he going to find the time to raise the two children she'd long ago stolen out of his life?

Not that he was any good at raising anyone. Look at the poor job he'd done of raising Ben after their parents had died. Ben had turned out to be all charm and little substance.

Shayne sighed, struggling with his anger.

How could Ben have done such a fool thing? Such a stupid, thoughtless thing? How could he have proposed to one woman—sight unseen—and then run off at the last minute because his ex-love Lila had come back into his life?

"I hope to hell you're enjoying yourself, Ben, because I'm sure not," he muttered under his breath as he made his way through the terminal.

The last place he wanted to be—the very last place— was the Anchorage Airport, looking for some woman who, if she did show up, probably didn't look a damn thing like the photograph he'd thought to take with him at the last minute. The one tucked away inside his pocket.

The photograph had to be a fake, taken of someone else, someone this "Sydney" woman knew. Nobody who looked that damn good would agree to marry a man she only knew on paper, a man she'd never met. More than that, nobody who looked that good would be willing leave civilization behind to come to what his late wife had referred to as "this godforsaken wilderness."

Shayne struggled to contain the impatience that mounted within him. Didn't he have enough to handle without this? He had two children in his life, children he barely knew. Children who looked at him with wary, distrustful eyes, probably because of all the things their mother had told them about him. Their divorce had been a bitter one. Bitter because he'd wanted her to remain, because he'd been so hurt that she could leave him so easily. Bitter because Barbara had taken off for New York and her affluent family without a backward glance, Sara and Mac in tow.

A court order, courtesy of an artful lawyer, had denied him visitation privileges. Her lawyer's justification: his visits, sporadic at best, would disrupt the flow of their young lives.

The one time he'd actually flown out to see his kids, Barbara had called the police. He hadn't even been able to broach the subject of having them come to visit him to Barbara, let alone the squadron of lawyers she'd employed to keep him away. Not wanting to pull the children into the center of the battlefield, and with no funds of his own to hire representation that even remotely approached the caliber of lawyers she had at her disposal, Shayne had retreated.

No, ''surrendered outright'' was more like it. But he'd never stopped loving them. His surrender had only had one term attached to it: that Barbara regularly send him photographs of the children. She'd reluctantly agreed.

The result: he had two children at home who didn't know him. Children he had to somehow incorporate into his life now that their mother was dead.

He didn't need to be out here, hunting for some woman who'd been foolish enough to believe Ben's silver-inked lies.

Didn't need to be out here, except that Ben had left him a note, asking him to do this ''one last favor'' for him. He supposed that he felt sorry for this woman and, in some remote way, responsible. Perhaps, if he had found a way to knock some sense of responsibility into Ben when they were growing up, instead of letting him slide, Ben wouldn't have done something this unpardonably thoughtless and cruel. Only three years older than Ben, Shayne had been no more prepared for the role of fatherhood at eighteen than he was now at thirty-four. But that was no excuse. He should have done a better job.

With an annoyed sigh, Shayne dragged a hand through his wayward black hair and looked around, feeling as if he was on a fool's errand.

People hurried by him. He looked at their faces, trying to make out features. He'd give this search half an hour, no more. There were far more pressing things waiting for him to tend to than looking for a woman who in all likelihood wasn't even here.

Part of him hoped she wasn't. He didn't relish having to explain this to her.

Shayne pulled out the photograph his brother had left with the note. Glancing at it again, Shayne shoved it back into his pocket, wrinkling it.

She wasn't here. He'd lay odds on it.

To be honest, Shayne had to admit a part of him had entertained the small hope that this woman Ben had been corresponding with would have a settling effect on his younger brother.

He should have known better.

There was no changing Ben. Not even medical school had tamed him. Why should a woman who was thousands of miles away make any difference to his brother?

But if that were the case, why had he asked her to marry him? What the hell had Ben been thinking?

That was just it. Ben hadn't been thinking. He'd just gone along with what had felt right at the moment. Running off with Lila had probably seemed right to him at the moment, too.

Ben's abrupt departure had squelched the last of Shayne's optimism. Not to mention removed the one buffer he'd had between him and his children. Ben had been the one highlight in their young lives since they'd been transplanted here two months ago. Mac and Sara both adored their uncle. He made them laugh and they could talk to him. Shayne didn't know what to say to them.

Shayne's mouth twisted into an ironic smile. When he and Ben were growing up, everyone had always depended on him, but it was Ben they had adored. Shayne had made his peace with that a long time ago.

So here he was, cleaning up another one of Ben's messes. The last one, if he was lucky.

Hers were the last two suitcases left on the carousel that displayed the disembarking passengers' luggage as it came off the conveyor belt. Instead of taking them, Sydney'd watched them go around and around as passenger after passenger subtracted pieces of luggage from the collection. It had given her an excuse to stay here, waiting in full view.

Her excuse was gone now. Everyone else had taken their luggage off. She couldn't just continue to stand beside the carousel, watching her suitcases move slowly around in a circle, only to appear time and again like the last two remaining wallflowers who hadn't been asked to dance.

Waiting until they reached her again, she took the suitcases off one at a time and debated what to do next. The logical thing was to remain in the airport until Ben appeared, or sent someone to get her. But she wasn't the type to stay put. She didn't like to wait, she liked to do, to move.

She thought of trying to locate a bush pilot who would be willing to fly her to Hades.

But what, if in doing that, she missed Ben? He could very well be on his way here right now. The idea of playing hide-and-seek between here and Hades was less than appealing.

They should have discussed an alternate plan, she thought. Too late now. Besides, it had never occurred to her that Ben wouldn't be here when she stepped off the plane. Everything he had ever written to her pointed to how reliable he was. Even the way he worried about his older brother, Shayne. He felt that Shayne had lost the ability to enjoy life, had allowed Alaska to deplete him rather than enhance him. It had begun early on, he'd written. Shayne had raised him after their parents had both died in an avalanche. His time to be young had abruptly ended. Ben's concern for Shayne was part of the reason she'd fallen in love with him. It just went to show her how large and caring a heart he had.

There had probably been an emergency for Ben to deal with, she finally decided. The clinic took up a great deal of his time and when he wasn't there, he was a bush pilot, flying supplies to people who lived and worked in even more out-of-the-way places than Hades. It would be just like him to put his own life on hold for someone else. In the short eight months that they'd corresponded, Sydney had felt that, with the exception of her late father and Marta, she had gotten to know Benjamin Kerrigan better than anyone she'd actually interacted face-to-face with.

It was time, she told herself, to do something before she grew roots in this airport terminal. Tucking her carry-on under her arm, and slinging her purse over her shoulder, she picked up her suitcases, ready to go in search of the information booth.

"Are you Sydney Elliot?"

The suitcases almost dropped from her fingers as her heart leaped to her throat.

Finally!

Sydney spun around in response to the gruffly voiced question, fully anticipating to see Ben standing behind her. As far as she knew, no one else here would know her name.

Her smile froze a little around the edges as a tinge of confusion took hold of her heart. The man standing in front of her resembled the man in the photograph she had in her purse, but in only the most cursory way. The man was a little older-looking, and... She supposed "harsher" would be the word she was looking for. His jaw appeared to be more chiseled than the one in the photograph, although that could be because of his expression.

The greatest difference was in the eyes. There was no laughter in this man's eyes. Instead of being the color of shamrocks in the morning, his emerald-green eyes were piercing, commanding. And troubled.

Something was very wrong here.

Sydney set her suitcases down, her eyes on the man's. "Yes?"

She wasn't as pretty as her photograph, Shayne realized. She was prettier, with hair like a golden sunset, eyes the color of the sky in the middle of summer, and skin the color of honey.

What was she doing here? he wondered again. Why would she want to live out her life in a place where most of the young inhabitants bailed out as soon as they reached the legal age of eighteen?

Sydney could feel his eyes boring into her, studying her dispassionately, as if she were an object rather than a person. The uneasiness within her grew a little greater.

She cleared her throat, hoping, too, to clear away her nervousness. "Did Ben send you?"

Even as she asked, she looked behind the man, praying that she'd see Ben walking toward her. But there was no one.

"Yes, he did." *Damn it, Ben, this was irresponsible, even for you.* The awkwardness of the situation chafed Shayne. There was no easy way to break this to her, and he'd never been much for talking. That, too, was Ben's gift, not his. "I didn't know how to reach you. By the time I found your address, you were already on your way here."

Her eyes narrowed as she tried to glean information from words that were just sailing past her without leaving an impression.

"I don't understand. Reach me about what?" She looked at him. "Who are you?"

"Shayne Kerrigan." As if in afterthought, he put out his hand. "Ben's brother."

The premonition she'd been sparring with scored a major hit and secured a huge toehold. Snatches of utterly opposing scenarios crowded her brain—Ben, taking the nearest dogsled out of Hades, escaping before her plane touched down. Ben, single-handedly fighting off some dreaded ebola virus. Ben—

She had to stop this. She couldn't keep speculating, not when there was a perfectly good way to access the information she sorely needed to calm her nerves.

"Why isn't Ben here?" She moved closer, searching Shayne's face. "Has something happened to him?"

Damn it, Shayne hated being put in this position. "Not exactly *to* him. But, yes, I'm afraid that something has happened."

The way he said that froze her heart. Iciness slipped completely over her, coating her skin with a thin layer of frost. Unwilling to let her imagination go any further, she placed her hand imploringly on his arm.

"What?" She wanted to know. "What's happened? Why isn't Ben here himself to tell me?"

Because he's a coward.

The words hovered on his lips, but Shayne didn't say them. He was loyal to the end, he supposed. Or maybe he was just stupid.

Shayne banked his annoyance. Ben wasn't bad, he just had this wild streak, a streak that refused to recognize that he was a grown man now and a grown man didn't propose to one woman, then run off with another. A grown man remained to sort things out and make them right.

When had Ben ever done that? The thought mocked Shayne. Ben had always relied on him to clean things up for him. Which then made this woman's dilemma his fault. If he'd instilled Ben with a better sense of responsibility—

But, damn it, no one had taught him that, Shayne thought. He just was.

Shayne looked at the woman in front of him, sympathy elbowing its way to the foreground. His tongue felt like a lead weight. "Ben can't be here himself," he said again.

Why was he toying with her like this? Sydney wondered. "Has he been detained?"

"No. Ben went to get married."

She smiled at Shayne then. The man was pulling her leg. All right, she could enjoy a joke with the best of them. "Yes, I know. Ben's getting married to me."

But Shayne shook his head. "Look, there's no polite, easy way to tell you this. Ben left a note for me early this morning." Shayne recited the essence of the note the way he would recite symptoms of frostbite to one of his patients. Quickly, dispassionately. "His old fiancée returned to Hades to look him up. The long and the short of it is, they patched up their differences and they're getting married. Might already be married, for all I know. He asked me to tell you.''

Sydney could only stare at him in disbelief.

Chapter Two

Shayne faltered when he saw the look of abject distress enter her eyes. And then her eyes began to shimmer with welled-up tears.

She wasn't going to cry, was she? Shayne felt something twist in his gut as he cursed Ben's thoughtlessness again. He'd never known what to do when a woman cried. Ben was the one with a talent for making them smile again, not him.

Shayne's inclination was to turn around and walk out of the airport as fast as he could. But he knew he couldn't. Wouldn't. One irresponsible coward to a family was enough.

Feeling awkward as hell, Shayne mumbled, "I'm sorry," then mentally fumbled, knowing that wasn't enough. He really didn't feel like having her make a scene here, not with him in it. But more than that, though she was a stranger to him, he didn't relish being the cause of her pain.

He wasn't, he reminded himself. Ben was.

"Ben isn't the most reliable of people," Shayne added after a beat.

"No," Sydney agreed, the words leaving her lips slowly. "I guess not."

She felt as if she were in a dream. A horrible, suffocating, recurring dream where she was moving in slow motion through a thick haze, waiting for things to become clear again. Except they weren't. And they wouldn't, not after what Shayne Kerrigan had just told her.

First Ken, now Ben.

Sydney blinked, desperate to keep the tears back. Served her right for putting her heart on the line again, she chided herself. Hadn't she learned her lesson the first time?

Obviously not. Well, she certainly learned it this time.

Damn you, Ben, Shayne thought. *Why can't you do your own dirty work? And why can't you ever try to live up to expectations?*

Shayne dug into his front pocket and held out a handkerchief to the woman. The flash of a smile she offered in return seemed to pierce right through him. He thought of Ralph Teager. He'd treated the man for the flu last week. Maybe he'd picked up the bug himself. There was no other explanation for the sudden quickening of his heartbeat.

Shayne shifted, glancing around the airport. No one seemed to be paying any attention to them. He wanted to keep it that way. Shayne looked again at the woman in front of him.

She looked a great deal more stoic than he knew

Ben's Lila to be. Birds of a feather, Ben and Lila. Both wanting to drain all the fun out of something, then move on. He hated to think of the kinds of kids they'd raise, if they managed to stay together long enough to have any.

But then, how stable could this woman actually be, he asked himself, dropping everything to fly out here to marry a man she'd never met? That certainly didn't bode well in the common sense department as far as he was concerned.

Oh, damn, she *was* going to cry. Helplessness seared through him, skewered him.

Shayne winced inwardly at the tears glistening in her eyes. He could see the struggle she was waging to not let them fall. Admiration whispered through him, quelling the helpless feeling. He admired control. Seeing it affected him far more than vulnerability. It was easy to go to pieces, to hysterically throw up one's hands and give up, the way Barbara had with life in Alaska. It was a great deal harder not to.

The woman Ben had abandoned went up a notch in Shayne's regard. She shouldn't have to put up with this.

He wasn't impulsive by nature, yet Shayne found himself sliding his hands beneath his faded royal blue parka and digging a worn and cracked wallet out of his back jeans' pocket.

"Look, why don't I buy you a plane ticket back to..." Shayne paused, waiting for her to fill in the destination. All he knew about her was that she had come from one of the other states.

"Nebraska. Omaha." Even as she said it, the city felt a million miles away from here. She'd left it all behind her in more ways than just physically.

"Omaha." Shayne nodded.

A nice, sane place. The woman should have had more sense, coming from the heart of the country. It made him think of grounded people, people with their feet firmly planted and their heads a long way away from the clouds. It seemed to him that someone there should have talked to this woman.

Opening his wallet, Shayne took out all the money he had on him and realized that it wouldn't be enough to cover a ticket. Resigned, he took out a small, folded piece of beige paper tucked behind the bills. It was a blank check that he kept strictly for emergencies. Unfolding it carefully, he told himself he should have known he'd use it someday to take care of one of Ben's problems.

Shayne glanced at "Ben's problem" again and couldn't help but wonder if she had no family, no one with brains enough to insist that she stay where she belonged instead of flying off to a place that probably seemed as alien to her as the moon.

"Why don't I buy you a ticket back to Omaha," he offered, "and you can put this whole ugly thing behind you?"

It definitely seemed like a plan to him. And this way, his conscience would be clear. But when he turned to go, he realized that Ben's mail-ordered fiancée wasn't beside him. Turning, he looked back at her, raising a brow in a silent question. Now what?

He struggled to not sound impatient. He'd taken precious time off he couldn't afford to lose just to be here. "Aren't you coming?"

It was tempting—oh, so tempting, Sydney thought, to take this man up on his offer, cut her losses and run back to familiar surroundings. But even though she'd left her best friend behind, familiar surroundings weren't enough. They wouldn't do this time. What she needed was a fresh start in a fresh place. That didn't include Omaha.

Sydney shook her head. "No."

He blinked, certain he'd heard wrong. "Excuse me?"

She took a deep breath. It was easier this time. "I said no."

Shayne thought he understood what the problem was. She was probably suspicious of the offer. After what she'd been through, he supposed he couldn't blame her.

He held his position, waiting for her to come to him.

"Maybe you don't understand." He held the blank check out to her. "I'm giving you your fare home. No strings attached. It's the least I can do after what Ben put you through."

It was also the most he could do because money was not something he had a great deal of. Enough for comfort, not enough for luxuries, and paying for a plane ticket for a strange woman came under the heading of luxuries.

Touched, Sydney crossed to him. She placed her hand over his and closed his fingers around the check. "Your offer is very kind, very generous, but I can't go back."

He didn't have time to argue. He'd promised to be back at the clinic by three. Removing her hand from his, Shayne tried to resolve the situation as quickly as possible.

"Look, if you're embarrassed to go home to your friends, I'm sure this kind of thing happens all the time." Although not to anyone he'd ever known, but Ben didn't have sole claim to being irresponsible. He couldn't have been the only one who had thoughtlessly left a woman twisting in the wind.

"More than you know," Sydney murmured. Even

though it had happened to her before with Ken, it wasn't embarrassment that was holding her back. "But you don't understand. I quit my job, ended my lease, and packed up everything to come here. I thought I was starting a new life."

So far, he didn't see the misunderstanding. "I appreciate that, but—"

"And I intend to start that new life," she insisted, raising her voice so he'd hear her above his own.

Exasperation sliced through his patience. How many different ways did he have to say this? "Didn't you hear me? Ben's gone. He eloped with someone and it wasn't you."

Sydney refused to let the pain his words aroused get the better of her. Instead, she doggedly continued as if he hadn't said anything.

"That new life will just be a little different than I planned, that's all." Sydney fought to hold a tight rein on her emotions. It wasn't easy.

What were the odds, she wondered disparagingly, of picking two losers in a row? Two men, both charming, both intelligent and attractive in myriad ways, who'd promised her the Hope diamond in exchange for her heart and then left her holding a tiny rhinestone in its place? Talk about being a lousy judge of character...

All right, from now on, she promised herself, she was going to stick to what she knew. Children. She understood children, could look into their hearts and know what they were about. That intuitiveness failed her completely when it came to men.

She didn't understand men who said things they didn't mean.

Shayne took back everything he'd thought about this

woman. She was as scatterbrained as they came. "And just what kind of life is that going to be?" he demanded.

Because he'd tried to be kind, Sydney didn't take offense at his tone. He probably thought she was crazy. He didn't understand how much she needed to begin again. Why should he? He was a man, a breed that didn't have problems; they just caused them.

She squared her shoulders. Directly behind him was a large bay window. Beyond it was a wonderland filled with snow, the sun gleaming off the ageless, pristine peaks of the Chugach Mountains. It heartened her.

"Alaska's a big, beautiful state. There has to be a place for me here somewhere."

"Oh, there're lots of places," he agreed. "But you'll most likely freeze to death in most of them." He looked at her. At first appraisal, she'd seemed fragile. Definitely not tough enough to make it out here. "Look, it takes a certain kind of person to move to Alaska."

He wasn't going to talk her out of this. She'd never been very malleable once she'd made up her mind.

"Well, for all intents and purposes, I've already moved up here, so it's a moot point. My things are on their way to Hades." The moving van had left the day before she did. She'd spent her last night in Omaha on Marta's couch, counting the minutes until her flight.

"I can tell them to go back when they get here."

And wouldn't the movers just love that? A round trip to Alaska, carting around her worldly goods. Her mouth curved mirthlessly. "They're liable to dump everything on the nearest snowbank."

"Alaska might be big, but there just aren't that many places for a woman to stay, not in a small town."

Ben had written to her about Hades, but he hadn't covered everything. "No hotels?"

Shayne laughed shortly. Hades was the very definition of small. Building a hotel was way down on the priority list. There were a few rooms over the Salty Saloon, but they weren't anything he'd recommend to a lady. "The town's not exactly a hot tourist attraction."

Sydney thought for a second, refusing to give up. "All right, what about Ben's place? You said he was gone." Pleased with her brainstorm, she picked up her suitcases. "I could stay there until I get my bearings."

And your brains, Shayne silently admonished. He took the suitcases from her and put them down again. "Ben doesn't have a place, he lives—lived—with me."

"I see." Sydney paused a moment, flagging, trying to regroup her thoughts. It seemed that there was an obstacle every way she turned.

As he waited, Shayne studied her face. Something in the set of her jaw softened him toward her. "You're determined to give this a try, aren't you?"

"Yes," she answered simply. "I have nothing left to lose now." She shrugged. Who knew? "Maybe I can still find that new life."

She had spirit, Shayne realized. It was coupled with stupidity, in his opinion, but it was spirit.

He refused to think over what he was about to say because if he did, he knew he wouldn't say it. As it was, he forced the words out of his mouth. "All right, you can stay with me."

Sydney had hoped he'd say that. But even as he did, she felt a little guilty. He clearly wasn't happy about the idea. "I can't put you out like that."

Picking up a suitcase in each hand, Shayne glared at her. The woman was turning out to be a handful. He really didn't need this. "Are you going to argue with me about everything?"

She didn't mean to sound as if she were arguing. "No, but—"

The almighty "but." Shayne turned on her, at the end of his patience. "Look, lady—"

"Sydney," she corrected, siphoning the wind out of his sails.

Sydney, he snorted to himself. That wasn't a name for a woman. It belonged to a man. In a pinch, to a city. But not to a woman with hair the color of summer marigolds and eyes the color of robin's eggs in spring.

"Sydney," he echoed finally. "If you want to stay in Hades, you don't have a whole lot of options open to you." He tightened his grip on the suitcase handles. "You either stay with someone who'll make room for you or you build yourself an igloo in the middle of town and set up housekeeping there."

She looked at him for a long moment, trying to read what was behind the stern expression. "And you'll make room for me?"

"I have room," he corrected. There was no point in her getting the wrong idea that he was going any more out of his way for her than he actually was. "Ben's room," he clarified. "So, are you coming with me, or are you going to do the sensible thing and go back to Omaha?" *Where you belong,* he added silently.

"I'm going ahead with my life," she answered. "Not back."

And with that, she turned toward the entrance of the airport, ready to face her somewhat altered destiny.

Already regretting his invitation, Shayne lengthened his stride to catch up with her.

They didn't have far to walk—Shayne had left his plane standing in the open field outside the terminal.

Sydney struggled somewhat to keep up because of the deep snow.

As she came closer to the airplane which looked small in comparison to the other planes around it, she could see that the diminutive Cessna had seen its share of travel. Sydney doubted that more than four people could fit into it comfortably. Maybe not even that.

She couldn't help but wonder if the old plane was safe.

Looking for something to say, she glanced at Shayne. He was behind her, tossing her luggage in under the rear seats.

"It's a nice plane."

"It gets me where I have to go," he said, not bothering to look at her.

Although, he admitted to himself, there were times when he hadn't been sure if it would. When he wasn't with patients, Shayne spent his time tinkering with the plane, trying to keep it running just a while longer until he had enough money to buy a new one. "Ben and I share it." A fond note entered his voice as he looked at the plane. They'd been through a lot together, he and the Cessna, and he tended to think of it in human terms. "I guess I should be grateful he didn't take this with him when he left."

Under the impression that Hades was only accessible by plane, Sydney had to ask. "How would he have—"

"There're a lot of ways to leave Hades if you really want to."

He'd seen her question coming. His guess was that Ben and Lila had prevailed on Jeb Kellogg. The general store owner's son was the only other person with a plane in the area. He could just picture Ben and Lila sharing space with ripened produce.

Abruptly, Shayne turned and slipped his hands around her waist to give her a boost up into the passenger seat. She felt even smaller than she looked, he realized, his fingers touching. The discovery almost made him lose the thread of the thought he was unraveling.

Leaning over her lap, he reached for her seat belt, then stopped. The less contact there was, the better. "Buckle up," he said gruffly. "This isn't going to be like the plane ride you just had."

No, Sydney thought several minutes into the flight, it certainly wasn't like the plane ride she'd just had. That had been smooth and turbulent-free. Shayne's plane vibrated and groaned as it strained to become airborne and leave the ground behind. Every motion reverberated through her body. Sydney felt as if she were on a ride in an amusement park. A very old, rickety ride.

Shayne glanced to his right and saw that she was holding on to the armrest between them. There was a glove on her hand, but he had no doubt that the knuckles beneath it were white. He was so used to this, it never occurred to him that she'd be frightened.

But she wasn't whining or screaming, he noted, approval slipping through him. Barbara had screamed the first and only time he'd ever taken her up in the plane. It'd been brand-new then. At least, brand new to him, he amended. She'd been horrified over the experience and even more horrified that he had used all his life savings to pay for a second-hand plane. Born in the lap of luxury, her father a respected surgeon at a renowned hospital, she'd counted on enjoying more of the same by becoming a doctor's wife.

Shayne knew he'd disappointed her in so many ways during their four years of marriage, but never more than when he'd told her he wanted to come back home to practice. She'd resisted the move with every fiber of her being, but he'd managed to finally convince her to give it a try.

They'd spent more months arguing about it than she'd actually stayed. Less than six months after she'd accompanied him to Hades, holding Mac's hand and pressing their infant daughter to her breast, Barbara had boarded a plane out. Not just any plane, but a summoned friend's private Learjet. Barbara had always had style.

Or thought she did, he added silently.

The woman next to him had less style but far more courage and class. He noticed that she'd ceased all attempts at conversation ever since they'd taken off. A closer look showed him that she was positively pale.

"You all right?" The question was gruffly asked.

People certainly didn't come to him for his bedside manner, Sydney thought. She didn't turn her head toward him when he spoke. For the time being, she didn't trust herself to look anywhere but straight ahead. She had this feeling that if she took her eyes off the flight path, they'd plummet to their deaths.

It was the same as when she'd first learned to drive a car. She'd been afraid to look anywhere but several feet in front of her. Except now, she wasn't piloting the plane, thank God.

"Fine." The answer whooshed out of her breathlessly.

He almost smiled at her reply. He'd been a little nervous, too, his first time up. Nervous and exhilarated. He loved the freedom flying gave him. "Takes some getting used to."

Ever so slightly, she nodded her head. "That would be my guess."

Her hands were probably like ice, even with the gloves, Shayne thought. He placed one hand over hers, offering her warmth. "You know, you can breathe. There is oxygen in the cabin."

Sydney felt silly. She'd been holding her breath without realizing it. Slowly she released it. Released, too, the armrest that she'd been squeezing.

She flushed. He flew this plane all the time and probably thought she was being an idiot.

"I've never been in a small plane before." Sydney took in a long breath and forced herself to calm down. "Actually, until I flew here, I'd never been in a plane before, period."

Shayne spared her a glance. In this day and age of frequent flyer miles, it was hard to believe that there was anyone left under the age of seventy who hadn't flown.

"Omaha that exciting?"

Excitement had nothing to do with it. A slight smile curved her lips. "No, I was just that busy."

"And now you're not?"

Sydney looked out to her right. There was only the slightest dusting of clouds, which looked like tiny bits of cotton pulled apart by eager, childish hands. She missed the kids she taught, she thought. A lot. She wasn't aware of the sigh that escaped as she murmured, "Not at the moment."

Seemed like a giant leap to come all the way here for a person who'd never flown before. "Why didn't you start out with something small, like a flight to Denver?"

She'd never wanted to go anywhere before. But after Ken had left her more than a year ago, she'd felt the need to get away, to find somewhere she could start her life over. Ben had offered her that chance. Or so she'd thought.

"Alaska seemed to have a lot more possibilities." She looked down, trying to envision the people who chose to make this land their home. "Everything just seems so fresh here."

"That's because it's refrigerated."

The remark, so carelessly uttered, amused Sydney.

Her laughter, sparkling with delight, surrounded Shayne unexpectedly. As did the strange, small wave that washed over him in its wake. If he didn't know better, he would have mistaken it for pleasure.

But pleasure had absolutely nothing to do with the present situation.

Recovering, Sydney blew out a breath. "After what you just told me in the airport, I didn't think I could laugh again." She turned to him, her eyes bright. "Thank you."

"I didn't mean it as a joke."

The denial, roughly voiced, had Sydney wondering if he had a problem accepting gratitude. He seemed nothing like his brother—at least, the Ben she'd come to know on paper. And yet she suspected that there was something kind and good about Shayne Kerrigan. It just seemed to make him uncomfortable to have someone else notice.

She smiled warmly at his profile. "Thanks just the same."

He said nothing in response, pretending not to hear her.

Chapter Three

"How much of what Ben told me is true?"

Her question broke the silence that had existed between them for the past several minutes. Silence that had only been interrupted by the intermittent rattle of a plane that sporadically insisted on making its movements known.

It took Shayne a minute to absorb what she was asking. He felt like a man standing in front of a minefield. It wasn't a situation to relish. Lately there'd been a great many minefields in his life, but they couldn't be avoided. This one could have been.

The ever-mounting list of what his brother owed him grew a little longer.

Shayne glanced in the woman's direction. Who in their right mind would agree to being a mail-order bride these days? he wondered again. At least she didn't look as if she was going to cry anymore.

"I don't know, what did he tell you?"

As she tried to gather her thoughts together to form a succinct answer, Sydney stared out the small window. There was nothing but a blanket of white beneath them, occasionally fringed with clusters of small wooded areas. Evergreens. They made her think of Christmas, even though the holiday was almost two months away.

"That you and he were born here. That you're both doctors and that he flew medicine in when he wasn't running the clinic—"

"Ben never ran the clinic," Shayne interjected before she could continue. He'd never understand why Ben, given to embellishing whenever the whim moved him, always felt the need to dramatize the truth, or depart from it altogether. Just being Ben should have been more than enough for him.

"The clinic belongs to me," he stated flatly. He'd used his own money to build it and had driven in a good many of the nails himself. "Ben puts in—put in—" Shayne stopped, wondering if Ben ever meant to return to Hades. His brother hadn't mentioned it in the note he'd hastily dashed off, only that he intended to snap up happiness when it presented itself and it had presented itself in Lila.

"He put in hours at the clinic," Shayne finally said. "He flew the plane more to entertain himself than to deliver medicine." That sounded a little bitter, he realized, though he hadn't meant it to be. "Don't get me wrong, when the going got rough, Ben was right there by my side."

"And when it wasn't rough?" She had to know just how badly she'd been taken in by this man's brother. How much of a fool she'd been.

Shayne shrugged. "He was somewhere else." And that, he had to admit, was most of the time.

In his letters, Sydney recalled, Ben had mentioned that he had a great many interests. She'd thought of him as a renaissance man. Now another image was beginning to form. Someone who enjoyed life and let his brother bear the lion's share of the responsibility.

"So he was a part-time doctor?"

That was one way to put it, but loyalty to his brother kept Shayne from agreeing.

"I don't think he ever really wanted to be one." Thinking out loud, he voiced a suspicion he'd kept locked up within him for a long time now. "I think he became a doctor because he thought it would please me." In a way, Shayne supposed, that made him even more responsible for the way Ben behaved. "And it did."

He remembered how damn proud he'd been of Ben when his brother had come home with his degree a year ago. He'd felt that Ben had finally grown up and, with Ben at his side in the clinic, he wasn't going to be alone anymore. His brother was going to join his practice and between them, they could do so much good. He supposed that had been all hubris on his part.

Shayne sighed. "Until I found out his heart wasn't in it."

The feeling struck a chord within her. Sydney pressed her lips together. "I guess his heart wasn't in a lot of things he did," she murmured more to herself than to Shayne. "Or promised."

He heard her. In an odd way, he realized that he empathized with Sydney. He knew how it felt to be abandoned. To feel so numb that you couldn't believe you were actually living through something so devastating, so appalling, or that you could go on living even when your heart had been ripped right out of your chest.

When he'd watched Barbara leave—even though he'd known that was what she intended to do—he hadn't been prepared for the emotional onslaught that followed in the wake of her departure. Hadn't been prepared for the horrid, gut-wrenching feelings that accompanied the realization that he hadn't meant enough to his wife for her to want to remain with him.

He moved the wheel, guiding the altimeter down a few degrees. "You'll get over it."

Sydney could feel her eyes growing moist. She couldn't let herself cry until she was alone. Gruff though this man next to her was, his kindness didn't deserve to be repaid with the tears of a sobbing woman.

She took a breath before she turned her head to look at him. "Excuse me?"

Shayne wasn't given to being talkative and wasn't good at articulating his thoughts. But she was in pain and he was a doctor. It was his sworn duty to alleviate the pain if he could, even if it wasn't the kind of pain that was found in any medical book.

"That feeling you have now—the one that feels as if something just kicked you right in your gut...you'll get over it."

He almost sounded gentle. She appreciated the effort. She had a feeling it probably didn't come easily to him. "Is that your professional opinion?"

Shayne stared straight ahead at the cloud formation. It was a perfect day to fly. "That's my personal opinion."

Had someone hurt him? She knew she couldn't ask. The way he said it, the topic was now closed. He wasn't about to tell her any more.

Ever so slowly, Shayne set the pace for the plane's descent. The small airstrip he'd forged was located just ahead, very close to his home. He'd done this so many times, the movements came to him automatically, without any thought.

He prepared to lower the landing gear. "What is it that you do when you're not packing up and moving to Alaska?"

"I'm a teacher." It made her feel less rootless when she said that. She was connected to the world by her work, by the minds she'd touched. That meant a great deal to her.

"We don't have a school in Hades." Which was something that hadn't concerned him one way or another until the past few months.

So many things that hadn't concerned him a year ago were now pushing their way to the foreground. He was responsible for two small souls. A responsibility that didn't end when he wrote out a prescription or doled out a kind word. It continued, round-the-clock, twenty-four hours a day. Waking or sleeping.

It was humbling and unnerving at the same time.

"There's one in Snowshoe, though." He did a quick calculation. "That's about thirty minutes from Hades— shortest route," he added. He didn't bother mentioning that sometimes, during the winter, the shortest route was completely impassable.

Sydney supposed that it was worth looking into. Maybe tomorrow, once she pulled herself together, she'd try to hire someone to take her there. "Do you know if they need a teacher?"

"No, I don't." He would have thought she would have directed these questions to Ben in her letters.

He knew very little about the school there, other than

that it existed. Right now, he was leaving his children's education up to the wife of the general store owner. For now, Shirley Kellogg was doing a fair job of it. The woman had received accreditation in a home studies program to teach her own brood of seven. With all of them grown now, she taught children in the area. He'd begun his own schooling that way, in a tiny log cabin that seemed old even by Hades's standards. Miss Faye had been the teacher then, and he'd learned a great deal.

But looking into the school at Snowshoe was something he was going to have to do soon, though. Mac and Sara were eventually going to need more education than Shirley Kellogg could provide just as he and Ben had needed. They'd attended school in the once-thriving town of Shelbyville, but it was now just a ghost town.

"What was it you were planning on doing after you and my brother were married?" he finally asked. Too late, he realized he'd opened a very raw subject. "Sorry," he muttered. "I didn't mean for it to sound like that. I'm not the talker in the family, Ben is."

"It's all right."

Sydney thought of the long letters Ben had written to her, planning their future. He'd envisioned them working together side by side. It was hard to believe that the plans had all been lies. Maybe there'd been a grain of truth in them. Maybe, if this ex-love of his hadn't shown up, Ben would have been at the airport to meet her and they could have begun this life together.

Hashing all that over in her mind wasn't going to accomplish anything, Sydney knew. She had to face the future, whatever that held for her.

She looked at Shayne, a thought coming to her. Maybe he could still use her.

"Ben said I could work at the clinic."

This was the first he'd heard of it. "Oh, he did, did he?" Just when was Ben planning on springing that one on him? In Ben's defense, Shayne realized he hadn't been very receptive about Ben marrying some woman sight unseen when he'd told him about his plans last week. He'd tried to talk him out of marrying a virtual stranger. Ben probably thought it best not to mention having her work at the clinic until after she arrived.

Of course, all that was water under the bridge now. She wouldn't be marrying Ben and as soon as she experienced a hostile winter, she'd be on the first plane out of here.

Sydney didn't particularly like the tone in his voice. The decision for her to work at the clinic wasn't based on charity or a nebulous whim.

"I have some medical training. I was going to become a doctor."

It was that, in part, that had brought them together. Ben had mentioned in the article what it was like, being one of the only two doctors for miles. He'd sounded quietly heroic and selfless. She'd fallen in love with that image.

Just went to show her there were no white knights left.

"What happened?" Shayne didn't bother to erase the skepticism from his voice.

The plane was rattling. Hard. Sydney wrapped her fingers around the armrests again. Her breath felt like a solid entity, weighing heavily in her lungs as the plane approached the airstrip. Her nerves jangled, mimicking the rhythm of the plane. She couldn't imagine wanting to do this over and over again.

Sydney forced her mind back to the question he'd just asked.

"My father became ill. The money I had for medical school went to take care of him." She'd never regretted that decision. But she did, at times, regret not being able to become a doctor. "Becoming a teacher seemed the best compromise."

She'd left him behind with that leap in conversation. "I don't see the connection," he said, flipping a lever, preparing the plane for landing.

"I was going to be a pediatrician." She was trying her level best not to sound as afraid as she felt. "I love working with children."

The short, soft laugh was self-depreciating. "You're a braver man than I, Gunga Din."

That caught her attention, drawing it away from the swiftly approaching frozen ground. "Kipling?"

He shrugged one shoulder carelessly. "I do a lot of reading. Not much to do at night around here."

"What does being brave have to do with children?" He was the brave one, flying this shaky tin can on a regular basis.

He thought of his children, two small strangers he had yet to get to know, much less understand. Almost every word out of his mouth seemed to be the wrong one. "They're just difficult to deal with."

Was it her imagination, or was the shaking lessening? She certainly hoped so. "No more than anyone else."

"I have no idea how to talk to children," he readily admitted.

That there should be a difference had never occurred to Sydney. She dealt with everyone in the same manner—honestly and with compassion. She supposed that, in the case of men, that was her mistake.

"Just the way you'd talk to anyone else," she told him. She watched the ground as it continued to approach them quickly. "Children surprise you. They're a great deal brighter than most adults give them credit for." The words dribbled out of her mouth as she braced herself for impact. "The trick to communicating with them is to remember how you felt when you were their age."

It seemed to Shayne that he had been born old. Childhood, if it had ever existed for him, was a million miles away. "I don't remember being their age."

His admission aroused her sympathy. "That's a shame."

He didn't deal well with pity. "If you say so." Shayne braced as the wheels of the plane made contact with the ground.

Like a dentist's drill that had slipped and hit a nerve, the jolt went through her entire body. Recovering, she sucked in a long breath to steady herself before she hazarded a look at him. He seemed completely unfazed.

"Do you always land that way?"

"No." Pressing the button, he released his seat belt, then wiggled it out of the slot when it refused to budge. "That was one of the smoother ones."

She thought he was kidding until she looked at his face. The man was dead serious. "Maybe you should get a bigger plane."

He was already out and ducking under the wing to get to her side. "I intend to. As soon as I can afford one." And from where he stood, that day wasn't going to be any time in the near future.

He held his arms out to her, waiting to help her down. She slid into them, realizing belatedly that her legs were shaky. When her feet touched the ground, they felt like limp dental floss. She sank as she tried to put her weight on them.

''Whoa.'' His arms tightened around her immediately, jerking her to him as he steadied her.

Something quick, sharp and elusive spiraled through her, discharging electricity like an eel that had been stepped on, the moment their bodies touched. Confusion creased her brow as she looked up at him.

The next second, the sensation was gone, vanishing as if it never existed. As if it were all in her mind.

Maybe it was, she thought. She'd been through a lot today and the day wasn't over.

Aware that he was holding her too close, Shayne loosened his grip. He peered at her face. ''Are you all right?''

She felt really foolish. ''Yes.'' With effort, she forced her legs to stiffen until they could support her. ''Just haven't got my sea legs yet—'' Sydney raised her eyes to his face. ''Or is the term 'air legs'?''

He wished she'd stop looking up at him like that. It made a man lose his train of thought. ''There is no term for it.'' He almost bit off the words. ''Can I let go now?''

To be on the safe side, Sydney kept a hand on his arm as she tested her legs before giving him an answer. Mercifully, they didn't buckle this time.

''They're steadier,'' she announced, then flashed a quick smile at him. ''Sorry, didn't mean to fall all over you like that.''

He'd had worse experiences. ''No harm done,'' he muttered.

But there had been harm, he thought. Holding her like that, however innocently, had only served to remind him just how long it had been since he'd held a woman in his arms. Up until this moment he'd talked himself into believing that it didn't matter. His practice kept him incredibly busy. And now, with his children here, he was *more* than busy. That was supposed to be enough.

It *had* been enough.

This wake-up call was far from welcome.

Abruptly, he turned from her and retrieved her luggage from behind the seats. He set the first suitcase on the ground, then leaned in to pull out the second one, setting it beside its mate as he secured the plane. Finished, he turned and picked up the suitcases. Snow clung to their bottoms as he grasped both handles in his hands.

Not accustomed to having someone else do for her, Sydney reached for the closest suitcase. But to her surprise, Shayne wouldn't release it.

"Here, let me take one." Sydney tried to reach for the handle again.

Shayne used the suitcase as a pointer, indicating the building in the distance. "Just walk," he instructed.

Since he couldn't be reasoned with, Sydney wrestled the suitcase out of his hand, then fell into step beside him. When he looked at her as if she'd just lost her mind, she asked pleasantly, "Were you in the army?"

Where had that come from? he wondered. "No, why?"

She grinned at him. "You sounded like a drill sergeant just then. I'm beginning to understand why you might have trouble talking to children."

There was no "might" about it. He had probably exchanged fewer than fifty sentences with Mac and Sara since they had come to live with him. And it was just getting harder, not easier, for him with each passing day.

Paying attention to what was in front of her, Sydney got her first clear view of the house where she would be staying. It looked exactly the way Ben had described it.

An old-styled, two-story Swiss chalet, all wood and stone perched on a tablecloth of pristine snow.

Sydney had a tremendous sense of homecoming, despite the extenuating circumstances.

"It's charming." Out of the corner of her eye, she saw the questioning look he gave her. "Your house," she explained.

Charming. Barbara hadn't thought so. She'd thought it hopelessly rustic and outdated. He'd promised to renovate it for her, but he hadn't found the time to get around to it. After six months, it ceased to be necessary.

As for himself, he'd never thought of the building in terms of adjectives. It was just home. It always had been.

"Thanks. Ben and I were born here," he heard himself unintentionally sharing with her, and shrugged it off to empathy.

"Really?" Ben had already told her that, but she pretended it was news. The house boasted four bedrooms and several fireplaces, she recalled. She'd thought it large for one man when Ben had described it. He'd promised that they'd fill it with children as soon as she was ready. The thought had thrilled her.

She couldn't believe that she'd been so easily taken in. With effort, she shook off the memory. "It looks so large. Were your parents wealthy?"

Only in terms of the love they bore one another, Shayne thought. Watching them, he'd grown up believing that husbands and wives adored each other and that marriage was forever. Finding out otherwise had been a rude revelation.

"No, my father was good with his hands," he explained matter-of-factly. "My mother wanted a large house. He wanted to please my mother."

"An admirable quality," she commented, shifting the suitcase to her other hand.

Shayne caught the motion out of the corner of his eye. Small wonder, he mused. It felt as if she'd packed rocks in both. Never breaking stride, he turned a hundred and eighty degrees, took the suitcase from her and then faced forward again. The expression on his face dared Sydney to offer any protest.

He noticed with satisfaction that she had enough sense to keep her mouth shut. They were at the front door quickly enough anyway.

Shayne nodded toward it. "Get the door, will you?"

"Sure." She turned toward him. "Where do you have the keys?" There was no Welcome mat before the threshold and she doubted if he meant for her to rifle though the pockets of his parka.

His eyes indicated the doorknob. "Just turn that, it's unlocked."

She liked that, Sydney thought. Liked the idea of living somewhere where she could keep the doors unlocked. Where she felt safe. But she had to admit it was going to take some getting used to.

Turning the doorknob, she pushed open the door and heard a startled, shrilled yelp from the other side. She immediately pulled the door to her before looking around it.

There were two children, a boy and a girl, standing directly behind it.

Children. Shayne had children, she remembered belatedly. Ben had written all about his niece and nephew. The affection that had spilled out in his words was just another element that had tugged on her heart and sealed her fate.

She left the door standing open as she looked from

one child to the other. "Oh, I'm sorry. Are you two all right?"

The boy, with his black hair and green eyes, looked like a miniature version of Shayne, right down to the scowl darkening his handsome face. His sister's features were far more delicate, her long, silky-blond hair unearthing the memory of a porcelain doll Sydney had once seen in a catalog.

"Yes." Huge blue eyes looked up at her as a shy smile made a hesitant appearance on the little girl's small lips.

There was no sign of a smile on the son's face. "Who's she?" he demanded of his father. It was obvious he was offended his father had brought someone into the house.

Instead of waiting for Shayne to make the introductions, Sydney put her hand out to the boy. "Hi, I'm Sydney. What's your name?"

"Mac Kerrigan." He gave the information grudgingly, though Sydney had the impression that he liked her shaking his hand. The green eyes swept over her critically. "Sydney's a funny name for a girl."

"You think so, too, huh?" Her agreement defused a little of his dark mood. "It was my dad's name. He gave it to me because he liked it so much." And because he'd hoped for a son, she added silently. The bond that was forged between them over the years, though, had quickly made gender unimportant.

Mac loftily accepted the reason. He jerked a thumb at the little girl. "This is Sara. She's my sister."

"Pleased to meet you, Sara." The girl's hand felt slight and cold in hers. Sydney glanced over her shoulder. She'd already made enough mistakes today. For all she knew, Ben had lied about the children, too. "Are they yours?"

"We're ours," Mac contradicted defiantly.

The boy had been growing steadily more hostile since their arrival. While Shayne understood that his son had experienced a lot of changes in his life lately, it didn't excuse his rudeness toward Sydney. It certainly wasn't making this ordeal any easier.

"They're my son and daughter," he answered, setting her suitcases at the foot of the stairs.

There was enough tension in the room to fill a sports arena, she thought.

Sara ran to the door, peering outside. "Is Uncle Ben with you?" she wailed. She turned to look accusingly at her father. "He said he'd be back soon, but that was so long ago."

"I told you, he's not coming back," her brother said to her, his young face etched with anger. Sydney couldn't tell if he was angry at Sara for believing, or at Ben for violating that belief. Probably a little bit of both. "He left us, too."

Too. The word echoed in the room, hurtful and sharp. Tears sprang to Sara's eyes as she hugged her doll to her chest.

Sydney turned to look at Shayne. His lips were pressed together in a single, hard line. She was beginning to see what Shayne had meant about not knowing what to say to children.

There was a definite challenge here.

Chapter Four

The misery in the little girl's eyes cut through any awkward feelings or decorum. There was no way Sydney could bring herself to ignore an unhappy child. It never occurred to her to even try.

As Shayne watched, surprised, Sydney dropped down to her knees in front of his daughter. Very gently, she turned the little girl's face toward her. Making eye contact, she smiled.

"I don't think your uncle Ben was thinking about leaving you, Sara. He was just too excited about getting married to realize that he couldn't keep his promise to you."

Sara's mouth formed a perfect *O*. "Uncle Ben's getting married?" She breathed the words in stunned disbelief.

"No, he's not," Mac insisted, elbowing his way between Sydney and his sister.

Sydney recognized it for what it was: Mac was being protective. For his own reasons, Mac was trying very hard to appear tough, but it was obvious that Sara was his weak spot.

"Oh, but he is," Sydney told him patiently. She looked from one child to the other, including them both. "To someone named Lila, wasn't it?"

She raised her eyes toward Shayne for confirmation. It cost her to talk about it so cavalierly, as if Ben were some stranger she didn't know instead of the man she'd come out to marry. But there was a great deal more at stake here than just her own feelings and wounded pride.

To be a child and feel abandoned had to be the worst of all possible worlds.

Shayne could only nod as he looked on. How could she look so detached, sharing something that he'd assumed was so painful and humiliating, for the sake of drying the tears of a child who meant nothing to her?

Maybe she wasn't nearly as upset about Ben jilting her as she'd earlier let on. In which case, he was being one hell of a fool, allowing himself to be suckered into letting her stay here because he felt guilty over what his brother had done.

He continued to watch Sydney in silence, trying to make up his mind about her.

Sara looked at Sydney uncertainly, vacillating between believing her and siding with her brother. "Uncle Ben was whistling when he left the house early this morning. I saw him," she volunteered, casting a side glance at Mac.

Sydney nodded. "That was because he was happy." She touched the little girl's cheek, affection already taking root. It didn't take long with her, she mused silently. She'd never met a child she didn't like. "He didn't mean to hurt you, Sara. Or you,'' she told Mac as she rose to her feet. She rested one hand on the boy's shoulder, but he shrugged it off. Sydney took it in stride. ''And he'll be back eventually, after his honeymoon.''

Sara stared at her, trying desperately to understand. ''What's a honeymoon?''

Something that she'd thought she'd be on very soon. Sydney blocked the thought. This wasn't about her, it was about two half-orphaned children not feeling as if everyone was leaving them emotionally stranded.

For their sake, Sydney forced herself to smile. ''That's something a man and woman go on right after they get married.''

Sara cocked her head, her brows drawing together. ''Like a vacation?''

Trust a child to cut to the heart of it. Sydney loved the way their minds were always working. ''Exactly like a vacation. A special kind of vacation for just the two of them.'' Sara's expression told her that, for the time being, the little girl was placated.

But the look on Mac's face indicated that he held everything suspect and was far from satisfied. Sydney had a feeling that he was probably more like his father than either one of them was aware of.

Turning toward Shayne, Sydney saw that he was looking at her as if he were working out a puzzle in his mind. Had she said something wrong, something to offend him?

But he didn't look angry, just…unreadable. And if body language was any indication of what he was feeling, he looked as though he was anxious to leave.

''Maybe you'd better show me where I'll be staying,'' she suggested.

Habit had him looking at his watch. Shayne frowned, letting his parka sleeve slip back down.

"Asia will have to do that." He'd used up more time than he'd realized. But that was because he hadn't expected to bring Sydney back with him. "I was due at the clinic fifteen minutes ago." He looked at Mac. "Where's Asia?"

Mac merely shrugged carelessly, a bored expression on his face. He didn't answer.

His insolence confounded and irritated Shayne, but before he could say anything to his son, Sara quickly volunteered. "She's in the kitchen."

In her own way, Sara was as protective of Mac as he was of her, Sydney noted.

"Asia." Shayne raised his voice to make it carry to the rear of the house.

Was that the housekeeper? Sydney wondered. It didn't matter, she didn't want to take the woman away from her work. The less waves she caused, the better she'd feel.

"That's all right," Sydney said, "if you just tell me which room it is—"

At that moment, a small, older woman walked into the room. She carried herself like a princess, her silver-gray hair falling in two long, perfect braids to her waist. As she approached, Sydney noted that her round face was the color of berries browned by the sun. The eyes belonged to a woman who had seen a great deal of life.

Her first real native Alaskan. The realization somehow made Sydney feel a little more familiar with her surroundings.

Eyes as black as midnight looked at Shayne, waiting.

"Asia, this is Miss Sydney." He gestured toward her.

"She'll be staying with us for a while. Show her to my brother's room, please."

Mac jumped on the words. "Then he's not coming back."

Sydney thought the triumph in his voice rang hollow. It couldn't be that Ben was the only one Mac had liked in this awful place he'd found himself transported to, could it? What about his own father?

"It's just temporary," Sydney put in quickly, sparing Shayne an explanation. "I'm kind of stranded right now and your father thought that until I figure out what I'm going to do, I could stay here. Since your uncle is away on his honeymoon, we didn't think that he'd mind my using the room."

Mac eyed her, uncertain as to whether or not he believed what she was saying. "When he comes back, you'll go?"

She heard the challenge in his voice. "I'll have to," Sydney answered simply. "There won't be any room for me here."

Maybe he *had* made a mistake, Shayne thought, upbraiding himself for his misguided invitation. She certainly didn't appear to be upset about being left at the proverbial altar. The woman sounded as removed from all this as if she were talking about an article she'd read in the newspaper.

Well, whether or not it was a mistake, he'd have to deal with it later. Right now, if past performance was any indication, he had a clinic full of patients waiting for him and no one to handle them.

He glanced at the housekeeper he'd been forced to engage with the children's arrival. Asia came from a village not far from Hades. He couldn't remember a time he hadn't seen her walking into town, trading goods at the general store. There'd always been several of her children in her wake. These days, the stragglers walking behind her were her grandchildren. She'd left their care to someone else to come work for him.

She wasn't a very good cook, and an even worse housekeeper, but at least there was someone here with Sara and Mac, which was what really counted.

"I'll be back after five, Asia."

Because their eyes met, entirely by accident on his part, Shayne nodded at Sydney as he crossed to the front door. A moment later the door closed behind him. He was gone.

She noted, uncomfortably, that Shayne hadn't said goodbye to either of his children and that they had made no effort to say anything to him, either. This was a family badly in need of mending.

"This way, please."

The softly spoken words roused her. Turning, Sydney saw that Asia was standing at the foot of the stairs, her expression completely impassive. She was waiting to take her to her new quarters, just as instructed.

Sydney picked up one of her suitcases and followed. "Coming." She forced herself to sound cheerful. It took a bit of doing.

Well, she thought as she followed the small woman up the stairs, she'd wanted a new life. This was certainly new. She was reminded of the adage that warned a person to be careful what they wished for.

"Have you been with Dr. Kerrigan long?" she asked.

Asia didn't bother turning around. "Not long."

"A month? A year?" she prodded, determined to at least get the woman to talk to her.

"Between." Asia went no further in pinpointing which it was.

She stopped at the second room on the right and gestured toward it. She made no effort to enter it, but merely stood back and waited for Sydney to open the door.

Why, was something going to spring out at her? At this point, Sydney decided she was braced for anything. Glancing at Asia, she reached for the knob, turned it, then opened the door.

Asia retreated a moment later, her mission accomplished.

Leaving the suitcase just inside the doorway, Sydney walked in. There was a stone fireplace on the far side and heavy wooden beams on the ceiling. The same kind of wood that made up the headboard and footboard of the large double bed. The room was as masculine as she would have expected it to be.

It was also in a state of complete chaos, as if its occupant had left in an extreme hurry.

As if its occupant had never bothered straightening things out to begin with, Sydney decided. She looked around slowly.

So, this belonged to the man she was to have married. Well, at least she wouldn't be faced with a lifetime of having to pick up after him.

The thought didn't do much to hearten her. Neither did knowing that, for whatever reason, she'd been made a fool of.

"Make lemonade, Syd, make lemonade," she muttered under her breath. It was something her father used to tell her whenever she felt as if she was faced with a horrible situation.

Sydney took a long, hard look around. She couldn't stay in a room that looked as though it had endured a lengthy visit from a passing tornado. Making up her mind, she blew out a breath and took off her parka.

The closet was as bad as the room, she discovered when she went to hang up her parka. What hangers were actually on the rod rather than on the closet floor were hopelessly tangled. Sydney looked around for somewhere to put the parka. Every available surface in the room was covered with clothing, books, papers.

How did the man ever find anything? She certainly hoped he was a better doctor than he was an organizer, otherwise she pitied his patients.

"It's messy."

The two-word sentence that came from behind her was hardly audible. Sydney turned to find Sara standing shyly in the doorway. The little girl was watching her every move.

Her first visitor. "It certainly is. But then, it's a boy's room and they tend to be messier than we are." The shared confidence brought a hint of a smile to Sara's mouth. Encouraged, Sydney ventured a little farther inside. "Would you like to come in? I think we can find a spot for you." To prove her point, Sydney quickly moved aside several thick sweaters from the foot of the unmade bed. She patted the cleared space, reinforcing her invitation. "There, how's that?"

Sara crossed to the bed. After a moment she hesitantly scooted onto it. Her legs dangled over the side. Sara clutched her doll to her, but she looked pleased by Sydney's attention. "Okay, I guess."

Sydney saw the way Sara looked around the room. There was loneliness in her eyes.

You're not the only one who misses him, Sara.

"There'll be more places for you to sit later after I clean up," she promised.

It was obvious that Sara was struggling to fit this newcomer into the scheme of things in this strange place she found herself. "Are you going to be the maid?"

Sydney laughed softly. She thought about curbing her inclination to ruffle the little girl's hair, then gave in. The curls felt silky around her fingers as she tousled them.

"No, I'm just someone who likes things neat."

Sara wiggled on the bed, settling in. She didn't seem to mind having Sydney touch her hair.

"We had a maid home." As soon as Sara mentioned home, the corners of her mouth drooped fornlornly. "Her name was Alice. But that was before...before Mama died," she whispered, fighting back tears.

Sydney looked down at the hurting little soul perched on the bed. "I'm very sorry about your mother, Sara." Sitting next to her, Sydney slipped her arm around the girl's shoulders. It warmed her when the child leaned into her. "Do you know she's watching you right now?"

Sara raised her head, looking at her with huge, incredulous eyes. "She is?"

Sydney nodded solemnly. "Uh-huh. From heaven." She pointed toward the window. Outside the sky was a picturesque, crystal-clear blue. You couldn't beat the view here, she thought. "She's looking down at you right now. And feeling very sad because you're feeling sad." The hope that entered Sara's eyes had Sydney going on. "Do you know, if you shut your eyes real tight and stay very still, you can almost feel her arms around you, giving you a hug like she used to?"

Sara looked a little skeptical. She was her father's daughter, all right, Sydney thought, even if she didn't look a thing like him.

"How do you know that?" Sara asked slowly.

"Because my dad's up there, too."

The bond between her father and her had been a strong one. He'd been her mentor and her best friend while she was growing up. An only child, she'd devoted herself to him when he'd become ill even though he'd urged her to go on with her life. When he'd died almost three years ago, she'd been devastated. Sydney supposed that was why she'd been so eager to fall in love when Ken had come into her life. She missed having someone to talk to, someone to share things with.

But Ken had proven unequal to the position—and unworthy of her heart. As for Ben...

Well, they just didn't make men like her father anymore. Attributes such as honesty and kindness appeared to be in short supply these days.

But even if they were in abundance, she was off the market, this time for good.

"And sometimes, when I feel very lonely and really, really miss him, I shut my eyes and remember how safe I felt when he hugged me. And then I can feel him doing it. Why don't you try it?" Sydney urged. She knew that when a child believed hard enough, anything was possible. "It'll make you feel better."

Sara took a deep breath, still a little uncertain. "I don't know."

"Why are you lying to her?" Mac barged into the room, glaring at Sydney accusingly, his hands curled into fists at his sides. "Why are you making up stories? Who told you you could lie to my sister?"

The intense verbal attack, coming from someone so young, took Sydney by surprise. But she'd learned to bounce back quickly around children no matter what they said. It was important to not lose newly won ground.

Instead of answering Mac, she looked at Sara. "I see you have a white knight, Sara."

Sara looked around, expecting to see someone else in the room. "I do?"

"Yes." Sydney gestured toward the scowling boy. "White knights go around protecting ladies, and it looks like Mac is your white knight, ready to do anyone in who messes with his sister."

"I am not a white knight," he protested.

Sydney noted that his protest was not quite as vehemently voiced as it could have been. Apparently he didn't find the image nearly as reprehensible as he was pretending. She'd work with that.

"Oh, but I think you are, and it's very nice of you, to want to protect your sister like that." She rose from the bed. The room wasn't going to clean itself and she was going to need all the time and energy she could muster. "But you don't have to worry. I wasn't lying to her. Your mother is watching over her. And you."

His eyes grew dark again. The momentary truce was over.

"She's not watching over anyone. She didn't care about us," he insisted. "She left us. Left us so *he* could drag us out here, away from our friends, from our home. I hate it here," Mac told her angrily.

Her mother had died when she was a little younger than Mac. Sydney remembered how angry she'd been at her mother for dying. Almost as angry as Mac. But she'd had her father to help mitigate the pain. And she hadn't been required to make the kind of adjustments that Mac and Sara had.

She tried to slip her hand around the slim shoulders, but he shrugged her off, just as he had downstairs. She pretended not to notice. "It's hard to get used to something different, isn't it?"

The small, firm chin rose defiantly. "I don't want to get used to it. I want to go home."

She understood, probably more than she'd anticipated. There was a part of her that wanted to run home now, too. Except that there was no home. Not the one she'd known. The same was true for Mac and Sara. That gave them something in common.

"Sometimes," Sydney told them quietly, "things happen and we don't understand why. But we always have to make the best of them. Otherwise, we just stay unhappy and then nobody wins."

Sara was hanging on her every word, trying hard to understand. "Is it a game?"

Sydney smiled at her. There were a lot of times she'd thought of life as a game. A game with ever-changing rules. "In a way. The winner is the one who's the happiest with what he or she has."

Sara snuck a shy look at her brother. He bossed her around a lot, but she loved him more than anyone. More than Mama even. She didn't want to be a winner if he couldn't be one, too.

"Can there be two winners?"

She was a honey, this one, Sydney thought. Unable to resist, Sydney sat down next to her again and slid the little girl onto her lap. Flimsy barriers melted as Sara gave in to her natural inclination and cuddled up against her. Sydney lost her heart completely.

"Oh, there can be lots and lots of winners, sweetheart." She stroked Sara's head as her eyes met Mac's. "The only loser is the one who refuses to try to be happy."

She felt pretty confident that, despite the way his lips

curled in contempt, she'd given Mac something to think about.

As good as Sara felt in her arms, she had work to do. Very gently, she eased the little girl from her lap again and rose.

"Well, I'd better get busy if I want to get this cleaned up before tonight." That definitely cut her work out for her, she thought.

Sara wriggled off the bed. "Do you want some help?" The question was tendered with hope.

Sydney knew how badly an extra pair of small hands could interfere. It went without saying that she could make more headway alone. But she also knew that Sara needed to feel as if she were part of something, instead of just standing on the outside, looking in. Sara and Mac both did.

And maybe, just maybe, so did she.

Sydney grinned at her. "I would *love* some help, Sara. Thank you for asking." It warmed her to see Sara puff up her chest importantly.

One down. One to go.

Turning toward Mac, Sydney was in time to see him pivot on his heel and walk out, his hands shoved deep into his pockets. Taking a chance, she appealed to the protector in him.

"Mac, I need someone big and strong to bring up my other suitcase. Do you think you could help me?"

Mac never slowed his pace, nor did he answer her directly, although she heard him mumble something to himself under his breath. Probably calling her a variety of names, she guessed.

This was, she thought, going to take time. But that was all right. She suddenly found herself with plenty of it to spare.

"Cleaning this room is going to be a big project," she said, turning back to Sara. "Why don't we start by picking up everything off the floor and putting it on the bed? That way, we can sort it out and maybe even get a glimpse of the floor." She looked around at the clutter. "There *is* a floor under all this, isn't there?"

"I think so," Sara answered honestly. She'd never actually seen it herself.

One arm tucked around her doll, Sara mimicked Sydney. Methodically, she began to pick up everything in her path, one at a time. Each item necessitated a trip to the bed, where it was deposited. Little by little, a scarred wooden floor that had once been buffed to a golden-honey sheen began to emerge.

Sydney wondered if there was anything around she could use to restore the shine. She doubted if Shayne would be of any help. Pushing that thought aside, Sydney decided to see if she could somehow untangle the mess in the closet so she could hang up some of the clothing closest to her. Enmeshed in wire hangers that had mysteriously linked themselves together, she was unprepared for the loud thud she heard behind her.

Not certain what she expected to see, she swung around. Mac was standing in the doorway, her suitcase in front of him. From the looks of it, he'd dragged it up the stairs with both hands.

"I brought it up," he said as if he expected her to dispute the matter.

"So I see." Crossing to it, she picked up the suitcase and carried it into the room. "Thank you."

His shoulders rose and fell indifferently as Mac retreated again, his scowl intact.

Sydney smiled to herself. That noise she heard was the first chink in the armor opening up. Promising, she mused. Maybe befriending him wasn't going to take as much work as she'd initially thought.

"You have a nice brother, Sara." She purposely raised her voice so the boy belonging to the shadow that fell across the hallway floor could hear.

"Mac's okay," Sara said in the timeless voice of sisters everywhere.

"Yes, he certainly is."

The shadow in the hall remained for quite some time.

Chapter Five

The moment Shayne walked into his clinic with its reception area teeming with patients, all thoughts about his chaotic personal life vanished. There was too much else to occupy his mind.

Shayne had always had the ability to concentrate on his work, his patient, to the complete exclusion of everything else going on around him. That was part of what made him such a good doctor.

And that was also part, Barbara had told him, of what had driven her away from him. She'd vehemently objected to not being the center of his universe. Coupled with having to live in a "frozen wasteland," as she'd scathingly referred to the region, she found his ability to successfully tune her out while he was working more than she could possibly put up with.

It had been the last straw.

Shayne looked around the clinic. Without anyone to

help out, he'd had a difficult time today juggling all his
patients. His last assistant had left over a month ago,
desperate to move on. The last he'd heard, she was in
New Mexico. So far, there'd been no new takers for the
job. Hades didn't have an endless supply of people. With
Ben no longer in the picture, Shayne was sure he was
about to fall headfirst into hell.

He thought about what Sydney had said about Ben
offering the position to Sydney, sight unseen, and he
could almost understand Ben's logic. Why not? His
brother'd offered himself to her under the same conditions.

Shayne couldn't help wondering, as he leaned over
and switched off the lamp on his desk, if Ben would
have really gone through with marrying Sydney had he
remained here. As far as looks went, he could have done
a lot worse.

A lot worse.

Tired, Shayne rose from his desk. He passed his hand
over his forehead and rubbed at his temples. There was
a tension headache building. Not from what he'd endured during the day, but in anticipation of what he was
about to face at home. Maybe he'd be lucky and they
would have all turned in early.

The last of the patients had left twenty minutes ago.
Office hours had long since been over. There were no
more traumas to occupy his thoughts, no continuing case
to baffle him and lay claim to his concentration.

There was nothing to face but going home.

Home to a houseful of people who made him uncomfortable.

Didn't seem right, he thought, shrugging into his
parka. A man shouldn't feel uncomfortable in his own
home. Crisscrossing a woolen scarf at his chest, he

tucked the ends in and zipped up his parka. Most of all, a man shouldn't feel uncomfortable with his own children. Raising the hood on his parka, he stepped outside and locked the door.

The cold air rubbed raw fingers over his face, stinging it as he got into his four-by-four and started the engine.

The wheel felt cold, even through his gloves. He'd never thought it would be this way. Whenever he'd envisioned his life, a century ago when he had dreams, he'd always thought there would be a wife, a family, by his side. A family who would give him all the warmth, all the support he had so sorely missed all those years he'd struggled to make a life for himself and his brother.

He exhaled and mist formed on the windshield. He rubbed it quickly away, shifted out of Park, and made his way down the familiar road.

Not that Ben and he hadn't been close. They were. But Ben...well, Ben was Ben. His brother had all the attributes he'd always wished he had. Ben had the outgoing manner that made people believe he cared about them. Shayne knew he cared just as much about his patients, maybe even more so, but for him, it had never been easy to show how he felt. Most people took that to mean that he was aloof, removed from them. After a while, it was just easier to let everyone believe what they wanted to believe. He busied himself in curing his patients, not keeping their demons away at night.

He supposed, Shayne conceded, it would have been easier to fall into that niche others saw him in and really not care. But he did. In his own fashion, he cared very much.

Cared, too, that his own children looked at him with either loathing or fear. He hadn't a clue how to cut through any of that. What the hell was he going to do now? he wondered as his snow-chained tires crunched through the newly fallen snow. Without Ben as a go-between, conversation with Mac and Sara would die altogether. There was no doubt in his mind that Mac somehow blamed him for Ben's absence, just as the boy seemed to blame him for his mother's death and for bringing him out here.

Maybe bringing them out here *had* been a mistake on his part. It was so hard to know how to do "the right thing." At the outset, it had seemed right. When he'd heard of Barbara's death, the first thing he'd thought of was his children. Of how they had to feel—scared, frightened, suddenly deprived of her love. Whatever else she had been with him, Shayne knew that Barbara had been a good mother to their children.

But now that they were here, in his home, he had absolutely no idea how to be their father.

High beams seared through the white world around him as he guided the vehicle toward his house. He tried to keep from thinking about how tired he felt. He knew from the accident victims he'd treated how easy it was to fall asleep behind the wheel, hypnotized by the sameness that existed out here. How easy it was to freeze to death.

The headlights from his vehicle bounced off his plane, standing regally in the field, poised to take off on its next run.

Almost home.

As he parked the four-by-four inside the detached garage he and Ben had built, he heard the roof groan under the weight of the snow as he closed the door. He'd have to see about clearing some of that off in the morning. If he remembered to get around to it.

Shayne looked toward the house. It was clear that the

children were unhappy here. Two months and they hadn't begun to adjust. Perhaps, for their own good, he should let his ex-in-laws take them. It wasn't something he wanted to do, but maybe it was for the best. The suggestion had been on the table when he'd flown to get Mac and Sara. To their credit, Barbara's parents hadn't pushed the matter.

Maybe they should have.

Standing on the front stoop, Shayne automatically stomped his feet. Bits of snow fell from the soles of his boots. Bracing himself, he opened the door.

The temperature change was a mild shock to his system. Pushing the door closed behind him, he heard the latch click into place as he opened his parka and looked around. At first, he saw no one in the room. A sigh of relief escaped his lips before he realized it.

Before he realized that he wasn't alone.

He saw her standing by the fireplace, the warm glow from the flames caressing her profile, getting lost in her hair. She'd undone it, he noticed. There was a great deal more of it than he'd first thought. It rained halfway down her back like a shimmering, pale gold shower.

His breath caught in his throat. The room was warmer than he remembered it.

When she looked in his direction, the smile that came to her lips in greeting went straight to his heart. He felt as if he'd just caught an electric eel, bare-handed. The tingling sensation raced up and down his body.

For one shining second, Shayne felt as if he'd stepped into someone else's life. Perhaps into his own life somewhere in that parallel universe where he was allowed to have the simple things that came so easily, so naturally, to other men. But not to him.

He shook himself.

Sydney had begun to think that they would have to go ahead with dinner without him. She'd already postponed it two hours and the children were getting hungry. There was just so long she could try to keep them entertained.

He looked so stunned, standing in front of the door, that she wondered if something was wrong. "I thought maybe an emergency took you away. It's been dark for a while." She'd heard him tell Asia he'd be home at five. Five had long since come and gone.

"It gets dark early here," he said matter-of-factly. "And sunrise is after ten."

About to remove his parka before he began to perspire, Shayne stopped to sniff the air. There was something tempting and delectable tantalizing his nose. Something quite apart from the light cologne he'd scented on her earlier.

He took in another whiff, still trying to place the aroma.

The puzzled expression on his face did a great deal to humanize him, Sydney decided as she stepped away from the fireplace. It almost made him look boyish, giving the hard, chiseled features more appeal.

She smiled in reply to the unspoken question in his eyes. "That's dinner."

"Not any dinner I've had in recent memory." Unless he and Ben went to the Salty Saloon, dinner usually consisted of whatever can he'd take it upon himself to open and heat. Asia had been put in charge of cooking when he'd brought the children to live here, but cooking was definitely not one of her strong points. Maybe Asia was picking up tips from her daughter-in-law.

"I took a few liberties with it. Asia looked like she needed help."

Because it seemed so natural to her, as she spoke she reached to take his parka from him, intending to hang it in the closet. She'd done this countless times before when her father had come home from work.

Except this time, she met with instant resistance.

Shayne held on to the parka. He hadn't brought her here to be a maid. "You don't have to wait on me."

"I wasn't aware that I was." To avoid arguing, she dropped her hands. "Although, in the strictest sense of the word, we all are."

He hung his parka on a hook, then turned to face her. What was she talking about? Who was "we"? "Excuse me?"

"We decided to wait with dinner until you arrived. It seemed only right," she added when he looked as if he didn't understand what she was saying.

Sara had told her that she and Mac usually ate in the kitchen by themselves. Sydney thought that was awful. Family meals were to be shared together whenever possible. So she'd talked them into waiting and entertained them as they waited. She read stories to Sara that Mac pretended to ignore.

Shayne looked at her suspiciously. Just what was she up to? "We, as in you and the children?"

She nodded. "Asia left shortly before five. One of her grandchildren came to get her." It had seemed like an emergency, and considering that the woman's idea of soup was warmed-over water with hunks of yellowed fat floating in it, Sydney thought they could definitely spare the housekeeper.

She saw anger crease his brow. Had she done something wrong in letting the woman go? There hadn't seemed to be much that she could do to prevent it. "I thought it would be all right since I was here with Mac and Sara.''

His eyes met hers. She was a stranger, Shayne thought. Where did she get off, letting Asia leave like that? He and Asia had an agreement. She was to remain with the children until he got home, no matter what that time was. He paid her accordingly.

''Making yourself at home, are you?''

Sydney wasn't sure if she was being challenged or not, and if she was, why. She struggled to keep her temper—something that had been badly frayed today—from flaring. ''Making myself useful.''

She was right. There was no reason for him to bite off her head like that. In all likelihood, she was just trying to help. He hung his scarf on top of the parka.

''Sorry, I'm not at my best at night.''

A smile curved the corners of her mouth as she cocked her head, studying him. ''Then that was your best I saw earlier, at the airport?''

He laughed shortly. She had him there. ''All right, this hasn't been my best day.''

Shayne glanced toward the alcove that doubled as a formal dining area on very rare occasions. The table his father had built with his own hands for his mother was set for four.

He didn't relish sitting across from accusing eyes. ''You could have had dinner without me.''

''I thought it might be better to have dinner with you.''

When he looked at her with another unspoken question in his eyes, she was ready for him. ''Your children are still adjusting to the change and to their loss. Any stability you can offer them will only help them with the transition.''

Terrific, Ben had proposed to someone who fancied herself a dime-store child psychologist. "You obviously don't know my children."

"No," she agreed, following him to the table. "But I intend to. Sara and I had a long talk while she was helping me clean the bedroom."

He stopped again, so abruptly that she walked right into him. He grabbed her shoulders to steady her. A second later, he dropped his hands, self-conscious at the unintended contact.

"Clean what bedroom?" He wanted to know. When he'd brought her here, he hadn't thought in terms of her doing anything, just staying out of the way until she changed her mind and left. He certainly hadn't bargained on her rearranging things.

"Ben's room. Don't worry," she said quickly, "I didn't throw anything out. I just sorted things and then stacked them out of the way. There's a lot more room to move around now." It hadn't been an easy feat, especially with the extra pair of small hands helping her. But she'd managed.

Wariness outweighed the sudden hunger that the warm aroma from the kitchen was creating within his belly. "What else did you do?"

It sound like an accusation, but she did her best to ignore his tone. "I already told you, I helped Asia with dinner. Actually, Sara and I did." She saw a little blond head peeking out from the kitchen. Smiling, Sydney held her hand out, urging Sara into the room. "Sara salted the soup, didn't you, Sara?"

Shayne turned toward the kitchen in time to see his daughter coming into the alcove. Her eyes on Sydney for encouragement, Sara nodded. "Yes."

Looking from his daughter to Sydney, Shayne wasn't

quite sure what to make of all this, or how he felt about it. Sydney'd certainly made more headway with his daughter in the few hours they'd been together than he had in two months. He was beginning to see why Ben had been attracted to her. They obviously had the same outgoing nature.

"Well, then, I guess I'll have to give the soup a try since you went to all that trouble, Sara." Shayne was surprised to see that Sara was fairly beaming at him.

It was, Sydney thought, like being in the midst of an armed truce. The silence in the room pulsed and throbbed like the vital signs of a comatose entity, giving no indication that it was going to awaken anytime in the near future.

Was this what mealtime was like in this house? No wonder Shayne had seemed unhappy that they had held dinner for him, if this was all he had to look forward to. But it took at least two for a conversation and he was as much at fault as the children. More, since he knew better.

She thought of the conversations she and her father had always had around the table. Dinner was when they could touch base, exchange ideas, share experiences. It was her favorite part of the day.

Here it seemed like catered torture.

She'd kept quiet at the beginning because she thought it wasn't her place to intrude into their traditions, whatever they were. But it was now obvious that there were no traditions to intrude upon.

Were they going to go through the whole meal without saying a single word? Sydney cleared her throat as Shayne set aside his soup bowl.

He looked at her quizzically. She indicated the bowl

with her eyes, an expression on her face he couldn't quite understand.

This obviously had to be what leading a horse to water was all about, Sydney muttered silently. She looked at Sara. "The soup was very good, Sara. I think the extra salt added just the right touch."

Was that what she was trying to tell him? That she wanted him to comment on the soup? Seemed rather silly to him, but Shayne took his cue. "Yes. It was very good, Sara."

Sara fairly beamed. She wriggled in her chair, sitting up straighter. "Mama let me help in the kitchen sometimes."

Glaring, Mac pushed his bowl away from him. "It's too salty." He looked at his father, daring him to dispute his declaration.

Sydney'd refereed enough playground disputes to recognize trouble before it exploded. "It might have been the fish," she quickly interjected. "You had that first," she told Mac, "and I might have added too much pepper to the coating before I fried it." She knew she'd done no such thing, but felt the lie was justified if she could avert a problem in the making. Genially, Sydney flashed an apologetic smile at the boy. "Sorry."

His mouth closed, the biting words on the edge of his tongue disappearing, absorbed by surprise. He wasn't accustomed to adults apologizing to him. Or even bothering to take note of his opinion.

Magnanimously, Mac lifted one shoulder, then let it fall again. "That's okay. The fish wasn't really that salty." His eyes shifted toward his sister. "And I guess the soup's okay, too."

Adoration gleamed in Sara's eyes. "Really?"

"I said so, didn't I?" Even at the tender age of nine,

Sydney could see that Mac was on his way to becoming a man, with a man's sense of the way things should be. Understated, of course, with little exposure of the emotions he entertained.

"Yes, you did," Sydney agreed before his tone could escalate and take the conversation off in another direction. She looked at Shayne. Other than the compliment she'd all but dragged out of his throat, he hadn't said anything. She gave it another try. "So, how was your day?"

"My day?" He looked surprised that she should ask.

"Yes. How was it?" She tried to seem nonchalant.

Shayne had no idea what she was going after this time and he was too tired to try to accommodate her. He cut a piece of the fish and ate before answering. "It was just another day."

Was it really this difficult for him to make conversation, or was he just being stubborn? "Did anything interesting happen at the clinic? Any patient stand out in your mind?"

He raised his eyes to hers. They held for a moment as he tried to figure out why she was asking him questions. Why should she care how his day went, or if his patients were interesting or not? They didn't even know each other. "No."

Pulling teeth was undoubtedly easier than this, Sydney thought. Doggedly, she kept at it. Ben had said his brother was a man of few words, but she hadn't thought it was this few. If ever a man had to be shown the way, it was Shayne Kerrigan. "Did you operate on someone?"

Mac leaned forward in his chair. The word "operate" triggered a memory of a program he'd seen back home.

"Did someone come in with a big, old fishhook stuck in them?"

"No." It was the first time that Mac had asked him a question that wasn't couched in total hostility. Shayne saw that his answer disappointed the boy. "Not today. But I did have someone come in last week with one stuck in their finger."

For the first time in two months, Shayne saw that he had Mac's attention.

Sara shivered and squealed. "His finger? Did it hurt?"

Mac looked at her contemptuously. "Sure it hurt, stupid. You try having a fishhook in your finger and see if it don't hurt."

"Mac, don't call your sister stupid," Shayne said sharply. There was no excuse for name-calling.

The fragile thread of kinship broke instantly. The moment was gone. Mac pushed aside his dish. "I'm not hungry anymore." He turned a defiant face toward his father. "Can I go?"

Shayne's inclination was to make his son remain at the table, but he knew it was useless to try to talk to the boy, to make him understand. Silently, he waved him away.

Mac fairly stomped out of the room.

Upset, afraid, Sara stared down at her plate, rocking to and fro.

"You can go, too, if you want," Shayne told her. He tried his best to sound gentle, but knew Sara wouldn't hear the tone, only the words. She was gone within the moment.

Sydney waited until she felt the children were out of earshot. Then she looked at Shayne. His expression was unreadable again.

"You shouldn't chase them away," she said quietly.

Annoyed at his inability to communicate with his own children, Shayne lashed out at the only target in the room.

"I don't recall asking you for an opinion."

She couldn't remember the last time she'd been intimidated by a dark look. Only incensed by it. "No, but that doesn't mean you don't need it."

Shayne pushed back his chair, the legs scraping along the bare floor. "Lady, I took you in because my brother did you a dirty turn. Don't push your luck."

"I'm not trying to push my luck. I'm trying to help you."

Rising, he threw down his napkin. This was shaping up as one of the worst days he'd had in a long time. "When I want your help, I'll ask you for it."

She was on her feet, too. "No, you won't." She knew that much about him even without Ben's letters. She could see the stubbornness in his eyes. "I see three people hurting in this house and since you're the adult, you have to reach out to them—to make the hurting go away—for all of you."

Shayne had always been a private man. He didn't like anyone intruding into his life. "Ben didn't mention you were a philosopher."

It took more than sarcasm to make her back off when she thought she was right. "I'm not. I'm a human being—and an outsider, so maybe I can see things that you're too close to see."

"Don't trouble yourself."

She raised her chin, determined to make him understand. "No trouble at all."

Just who the hell did she think she was, spouting off solutions as if she somehow had turned to the last page of his life, where all the answers were supposed to be written?

Shayne blew out a breath, getting hold of himself. He hadn't meant to lose his temper like that. And maybe she had a point. God knew, he wasn't making any headway with Mac and Sara up until now. This tiny spate of conversation at the table tonight had been the longest one they'd enjoyed.

He eyed Sydney in pensive silence. She was obviously better at this sort of thing than he was. "You got Sara to help you?"

Sydney nodded. "Actually, she volunteered. Mac carried up my suitcase."

Shayne found that almost impossible to believe. Mac was like a brick wall. Even Ben had found it difficult to get the boy to open up.

"Mac?"

"Mac," she confirmed, a small smile of triumph playing on her lips.

"How about that," he murmured.

Maybe there was a place for minor miracles, after all. Shayne rubbed his neck, wondering if it had been just a fluke, or if all it took to open his son up was patience—and the right approach. An approach she seemed to have a lock on.

The antique mantel clock that had been passed down in his mother's family for generations chimed eight o'clock. Early by most standards. Late by the hours he kept. He looked at Sydney and thought she looked tired. She could probably use the rest after what she'd been through.

"It's been a long day. Why don't you call it a night and turn in?"

Sydney raised a brow, amused. "Sending me to my room?"

She could go or stay, it was all the same to him. He had some reading to catch up on. "Just making a suggestion."

"And in this case, a good one." There were dishes on the table, but Sydney felt suddenly drained. Besides, he'd said he didn't want her waiting on him. That undoubtedly included clearing the table, as well. She'd leave that to him. "I think I will go to bed." She turned to leave the room.

She heard the clink of dishes behind her. He was gathering them together. Sydney stopped. "Want help with that?"

"No."

"Why doesn't that surprise me?" she said more to herself than to him. She was at the foot of the stairs when he called to her.

"Ms. Elliot."

Pausing, she looked at him over her shoulder. "Yes?"

Shayne kept his eyes on the dishes he was stacking. He'd been downright uncivil to her and he knew it. It wasn't her fault that she'd wandered into a demilitarized war zone. Under the circumstances, she was doing her best to get along.

"For what it's worth, I think Ben missed out."

He probably had no idea how much she needed to hear something like that, Sydney thought. Or how good it sounded. She smiled her appreciation, even though it was to the top of his bent head.

"Thank you."

Shayne didn't bother saying anything to her in response. As far as he was concerned, he'd already said too much.

Chapter Six

Sighing, Shayne closed his book. There was no point in sitting here, trying to make sense out of the words in front of him. He'd been on the same page for the past fifteen minutes, reading it over and over again. None of it was sinking in.

His mind just wasn't on Dumas or his novel about the prince history had chosen to hide. Rising from his chair, Shayne crossed to one of the two bookshelves that buffered the fireplace and returned the leather-bound volume to its place. Tonight it had failed to transport him beyond his four walls.

Normally, when the long night wrapped itself tightly around him, Shayne found he could loosen the day's tension by losing himself in the pages of the books he'd been collecting over the years.

But tonight was different. Tonight nothing could erase the unease he was feeling. Unease mingled with dissatisfaction and a restlessness that seemed to have no reason behind it, no identifying marks for him to trace with confidence to its source.

A restlessness that had begun the moment he'd walked into his house and seen Sydney standing by the fireplace. If he closed his eyes, he could still see her, looking every bit the embodiment of a dream he'd once deluded himself into having. A dream of hearth and home. And family.

He was far too much of a realist now to believe in dreams. That had belonged to the remnants of the child in him. A child who had long since grown up to face the world for what it was. A hard, exacting place that never allowed you to put your guard down.

The restlessness refused to recede.

Instead, it threatened to swallow him up. Maybe he was just reacting to Ben's latest escapade, an escapade that left him—however temporarily—not only without another pair of skilled hands at the clinic, but with a woman he hadn't the slightest idea what to do with.

The ratio out here being seven to one, he knew there would be a lot of men who'd offer very vocal suggestions as to what he *could* do with Sydney, but Shayne'd never been one for casual coupling. Which was why Barbara had hurt him as much as she had.

He supposed if he were a drinking man, he would have tried to lose himself inside a bottle tonight. But even if he were so inclined, he didn't have that luxury available to him. A doctor out here couldn't afford to drink and muddle his mind. Especially if he were the only doctor in a hundred-mile radius—and it looked like he was, at least for the time being.

So, he had no crutches to lean on, no quick fixes at

his disposal, other than his books, and they just weren't doing the trick tonight.

Sleep was the only solution left.

If he could sleep, he thought, agitation rippling through him like a freshly caught salmon thrown on the ground.

With careful movements, he banked the fire in the fireplace. Then, one by one, he switched off the lights until only the upstairs hallway light filtered down to him like a thin, winding golden thread.

He took the stairs slowly, his thoughts involuntarily straying to the woman whom he presumed was now fast asleep. How long was she going to stay here? God, he hoped not long. He had enough on his mind without having to put up with any of Ben's fallout.

He could hear the branches scraping against the upstairs hall window. The wind had been picking up steadily all evening and now mournfully strummed the branches of the surrounding trees. It only added to his restlessness.

Stopping at the landing, Shayne glanced toward the bedrooms opposite his own. Sara's and Mac's bedrooms. Every night, before he went to bed, he looked in on them, always when he was certain they were asleep.

At first, it had been out of pure amazement, to assure himself that, after all these years of separation, they were actually finally here in his house. Now it was a habit, something he did before closing the door to his own room. He wasn't even sure why he did it, only that he needed to, needed to see their faces, peaceful and devoid of any emotions directed against him, pressed softly against their pillows.

He eased open Mac's door first. The boy was on his stomach, his blanket a hopeless tangle at his feet. He slept like a spinning top. Very gently, Shayne freed enough of the blanket to spread over the wiry body. Mac slept like Ben, turning his bed into a huge battlefield as he sought out sleep. The thought made Shayne smile as he withdrew from the room.

Approaching Sara's room, Shayne thought he heard the soft murmur of a woman's voice. *Her* voice. Was he imagining it? He listened again. It sounded too real to be his imagination. Curious, he eased the door open.

Sara was in bed, her eyes shut, her hand curled around Sydney's. She looked sound asleep. What was Sydney doing in the room with her?

And then he saw that there was an open book on Sydney's lap. One of Sara's storybooks.

She'd heard him the moment he opened the door. Turning, she put her finger to her lips, afraid, he realized, that he would say something to wake Sara up. He watched as she looked at Sara again—apparently to satisfy herself that the little girl was still asleep—then, very slowly, eased her hand from Sara's.

It was like watching someone move in slow motion, he thought. Every movement was fluid, unhurried. A little like poetry on a soft summer's night. He found himself almost hypnotized, hardly breathing until, tiptoeing out of the room, she came to him.

Belatedly, Shayne backed up to give her room until they were both standing out in the hallway. Sydney closed the door quietly behind her, turning so that her body was a breath away from his.

And one breath too close.

Shayne didn't step back, not immediately, though he knew he should. Instead, in a hushed voice gauged not to wake either child, he asked, ''What were you doing in her room?''

Sydney thought it was obvious, but she explained anyway. "Sara had a nightmare. I heard her whimpering in her sleep so I went in and woke her up. She was terrified, something to do with thunder and her mother dying." The little girl's eyes had looked haunted until she'd managed to calm Sara down. "I didn't get it all. But whatever it was about, the nightmare was enough to make her afraid. I promised to stay with her until she fell asleep again. I figured the quickest way to make that happen was to read to her." Sydney grinned, tapping the book she held in her hand. "Works every time."

How many children had she read to sleep? Shayne wondered. And why didn't she have any of her own? Was there more to this woman than met the eye? He still couldn't get himself to believe that a woman as vibrant as Sydney Elliot had conducted a long-distance mail romance with a man she'd never met. Surely she'd have to have men in closer proximity in her life. Where were they?

"I didn't hear her," he confessed.

"It was a whimper, not a scream." Her words were swallowed by the rattle of the windows as they trembled before the wind. "And that sounds pretty fierce." She nodded in the general direction of the windows on his side of the house. "It would have blotted out even a loud whimper. Besides, my room's next to hers," Sydney added. "I could hear her better than you could."

Shayne knew he should be grateful to her for going to Sara, not subjecting her to the third degree. It was just that he wasn't accustomed to anyone helping him. He was always on the giving end, not the receiving one. "Thank you for taking care of her."

She smiled, erasing the tension of suspicion and inadvertently creating a whole different kind of tension in its wake.

It was obvious that words of thanks came hard to him, Sydney realized. "No hardship. As I said earlier, I like kids and I enjoy being in their company."

That settled, there seemed to be nothing more to say. Yet, he couldn't seem to make himself withdraw, not just yet. So he remained where he was, feeling awkward, like some bump in the rug, unable to move away. She wasn't helping, looking up at him like that, her eyes as warm as the sea in July.

Shayne cleared his throat, as if that would somehow help to clear his mind, as well. It felt muddled now. He couldn't seem to focus on a complete thought. Was he *that* tired?

"Have you given any thought to what you want to do? I mean, about finding work? If you're serious about staying, that is."

This wasn't coming out at all well. He'd never been particularly articulate in private, but if he continued in this backward evolutionary spiral, he was going to be reduced to a Neanderthal, making unintelligible sounds and grunts by morning.

It seemed to Sydney that they should have had this conversation earlier at the dinner table, when she'd tried to pry words out of his mouth. When she was fresher.

"I was hoping that maybe the job that Ben mentioned might still be open." Was that being presumptuous on her part? Shayne hadn't seemed very pleased when she'd mentioned earlier that Ben wanted her to work at the clinic.

Shayne thought of his day and how exhausted he'd become trying to do everything while patients poured into the clinic like the aftermath of a flash flood. He supposed he had nothing to lose by hiring her, at least on a trial basis. She certainly seemed willing enough to work and she was better than nothing.

His eyes drifted over the length of her. Sydney was wearing a silk robe that insisted on molding itself to her every movement like a second, shimmering peach skin.

Definitely better than nothing, he thought.

The restlessness within him intensified, blatantly hinting at its source.

Shayne banked the fire that leaped into his veins, just as he'd banked down the one in his den. It was late and he was tired. It was time to end this conversation.

"It's open, all right. I suppose we could give it a try for a few days, see how things work out. I usually go in at eight."

"Eight's fine," Sydney said quickly.

"Asia's here by seven. She sees to Mac and Sara while I'm gone." The words came out double-time, as if he were a military leader, snapping out orders. He had no idea why he was even bothering with the extra information. It wasn't necessary. She didn't need to know any of it. Yet he'd found himself elaborating.

"I don't mean to pry, but what about their education?"

He almost laughed. For a woman who didn't mean to pry, she certainly seemed very good at it. This wasn't any of her business.

"They're getting one," he assured her formally. "Asia takes them into town. Shirley Kellogg, the general store owner's wife, teaches the kids from the area for three hours a day."

"Three hours?" That didn't seem like very much, especially if the children were rowdy. In her experience, that meant most of the time would be spent refereeing.

How much could they really learn in that kind of atmosphere?

Shayne knew criticism in the offing when he heard it. "That's all that's needed, if it's done correctly."

Sydney had thoughts on that subject, but knew that, for the time being, if she wanted the job with Shayne, it was best to keep those thoughts to herself. "You may have a point," she conceded.

Taking advantage of the momentary break in conversation, Shayne turned on his heel before she could say anything else to keep him standing out here, entertaining thoughts that had no business existing. "I'll see you in the morning."

"In the morning," she echoed.

Eight wasn't fine, no matter what Sydney had said the night before, she groggily realized as the alarm went off. And if eight wasn't fine, that made six-thirty even less so.

When she'd agreed to the time, it had been from the comfortable side of an evening when she'd been wide awake and eager to get her life in gear and moving forward. It was a whole different matter now.

Despite her chosen vocation that required her to rise early, Sydney had never been a morning person. She faced it reluctantly, as a necessary evil to endure. An obstacle to overcome and vanquish—like a medieval dragon. Her absolute rock bottom requirement in facing such an early hour was that there be some semblance of daylight to make the passage from bed to bathroom acceptable and civilized.

There wasn't even any daylight. In fact, there was no light to speak of outside her window at all.

This had to be a mistake. The alarm clock had to have gone off by mistake, she thought groggily.

Her brain in a fog, Sydney groped for the alarm clock she'd brought with her, flirting with the idea of dropping it on the floor once she found it. As if in a desperate play for survival, the clock defied detection, continuing to ring, violently shredding the darkness that surrounded her.

The noise throbbed in her head like a headache in the making.

And then she heard the door to her room opening. Light from the hallway came spilling in, ushering with it a small, nightgown-shrouded form.

"Sydney? Are you up?"

Still more than half-asleep, Sydney raised her head from her pillow, focusing on the source of the voice. Slowly, the form solidified.

Sara.

It took almost superhuman effort, but Sydney managed to sit up and drag her hair, if not sleep, from her eyes. She released a long, shaky breath.

"I am now, sugar."

Sara peered nervously into the room. "What's that noise?" Hesitantly, she ventured into the room.

Focusing her eyes, Sydney finally zeroed in on the clock. Bracing one hand against the bed, she reached over and shut the alarm off. Finally!

Sydney settled back against the headboard. "That is something I bought to annoy myself."

It didn't make any sense to Sara, but she liked Sydney and she wanted to understand. "Why?"

"Long story." Sara's puzzled expression made her laugh softly. "It's an alarm clock, honey. I set it so it can wake me up." She sighed, knowing that there was no way she could go back to sleep now. "I have trouble waking up in the morning."

Sara thought the confession over for a moment. "I could come in and wake you up in the morning if you want me to." She rocked on her toes, eyeing Sydney to see how she liked her suggestion.

"And probably do a much nicer job than that old clock," Sydney agreed. She smiled at the girl. "That's very generous of you, Sara. Maybe I'll take you up on that."

Appearing pleased at the compliment, Sara asked, "Are you going to stay here with us today, too?"

The hope in the girl's voice touched Sydney. "No, I'm going in with your father and work at the clinic, but I'll be back tonight."

"You're going to work there like Uncle Ben?"

"Not exactly. I'm not a doctor." Sydney wasn't aware of the wistfulness in her voice until she heard it herself.

"I bet you could be if you wanted to."

Sydney couldn't resist. She pulled the girl to her and hugged her.

Sara squealed and giggled, purely delighted. Sydney hugged her harder, which only made Sara laugh louder.

Impulsively, Sara kissed her on the cheek.

Sydney completely lost her heart to the little girl. She brushed a kiss against the silky head. "Thank you, Sara. I needed that. I was running really low on hugs."

Sara scrambled up on her knees on the bed. "Do you need hugs?"

"Everybody needs hugs." Some people just didn't know it. Sydney had a feeling the good doctor fell into that category. "Don't you?"

Looking surprised at being found out, Sara nodded

vigorously, the ends of her hair bobbing up and down like tiny springs. "Yes, but everybody doesn't need them. Mac says he doesn't. And my daddy doesn't."

"Oh, I think you're wrong there. Mac and your daddy both need them. As a matter of fact, I think your daddy needs them most of all." She saw the doubt in Sara's eyes as she reached for her robe, not that it offered much protection from the cold. "He just doesn't know how to ask. Tell you what—" Sydney swung her legs over the side of the bed and rose "—why don't you hug him when you go downstairs?" She slipped the robe on over her arms and tied the sash. "It'll be a nice surprise for him."

Sara cocked her head, mulling the suggestion over. "You think?"

Sydney ruffled her hair, laughing. "I think."

Shayne glanced at his watch, wondering if he should go and wake Sydney, or just leave when he said he would. It was almost seven-thirty. Sydney should have been down here by now if she was coming with him to the clinic. Probably sleeping in, he guessed. Morning without dawn took some getting used to. He had no doubt that her system was also thrown off by the time change she'd experienced, coming from Nebraska.

Just as well. The woman would probably only get in the way instead of help. The last thing he needed was someone getting in his way.

The bottom step squeaked. Hearing it, Shayne turned around. But instead of Sydney, he found himself looking down into his daughter's face. Mac was probably still upstairs—avoiding him, like most mornings.

"Good morning, Sara."

"Good morning," she echoed, then tugged on his sleeve and beckoned him down to her level.

Not knowing what to expect, he knelt. "Something wrong, Sara?"

She didn't answer. Instead she caught her lower lip between her teeth, worrying it a little. Then she put her small arms as far around him as she could and squeezed. Hard.

Startled, it took Shayne a moment before he responded. Had something happened? Was she afraid? But when he tilted Sara's head back slightly to look at her, none of that was evident in her face. She looked a little nervous, but that was all.

"What's this all about?"

Sara wondered if maybe she was doing it wrong. Did grown-ups hug different? "I'm hugging you, Daddy."

"Yes, I know, but why?"

This had come completely out of the blue. Sara hadn't hugged him when she'd first met him, and after that, there'd been no reason to. At least none that he could see. There still wasn't. For that matter, she hadn't called him Daddy before, either. The last time he'd seen her, she was six months old. To her, he was more of a stranger than "Daddy."

An impatient little frown creased her small mouth. Didn't he like being hugged? Was Sydney wrong? "Because Sydney said you needed one."

"Oh, she did, did she?" Sydney took a lot upon herself, especially for a stranger, he thought. He had to admit, though, this once couldn't find fault with that. "I guess she's right."

Like a man picking his way across a sheet of ice he knew was dangerously thin, Shayne lightly stroked his daughter's hair. Emotions too large and unwieldy to be captured and caged slammed through him, making holes, creating chasms. Leaving him stunned by their intensity. He had no idea just how much he'd missed having his children with him, missed having their love, until this very moment.

He held Sara to him, wondering how someone so small could be responsible for creating something so immense. Like a huge net, love spread completely over his heart, enmeshing it.

Wrapped up in this newly roused emotion, it took Shayne a few minutes to realize that he was no longer alone in the room with Sara. Raising his eyes, he saw Sydney in the doorway, a pleased smile on her lips as she watched them. He hadn't even heard the bottom step squeak.

Emotion quickened in his throat. He tried to clear it away. "I'm told I have you to thank for this."

Sydney raised one shoulder, letting it drop again. "The only one you have to thank is Sara." She looked toward the kitchen. There was no telltale aroma in the air. "Any breakfast ready? If not, I could whip up something."

He had no doubt that she could. And breakfast was only part of it. Surprised by the stray thought, he wondered where it had come from. "There's no need. Asia's taking care of it."

Asia. Sydney thought of last night's soup before she'd put her hand to it. Food for survival, not for enjoyment. She didn't think she was up to facing that this early. A sunless morning was difficult enough.

She began to edge her way out of the room. "I'll just go see if she needs any help."

He knew it was useless to tell her not to bother. She

didn't seem to be the type who listened to things she didn't want to hear. For now, he let it go.

Sara watched Sydney leave the room, then looked up at her father. "I like her," she pronounced. When he said nothing, she cocked her head, studying him. "Do you like Sydney?"

He knew she wanted him to say yes, but he wanted to be truthful with her at all times. That way, she'd never have cause to doubt him.

"I don't know yet." He looked down again at Sara's face.

She was smiling at him, her young eyes sparkling as if there were some delicious secret dancing inside of her. He had never seen them look so bright, so lively. He gave in to the feeling coursing through him and hugged Sara again. Sara nestled happily against him.

What he did know, he thought, was that this woman Ben had brought into their lives was apparently someone who knew what she wanted and went after it. As far as traits went, it wasn't a bad one to have.

As long as it didn't get in his way.

Chapter Seven

"And what's your problem?"

The question sounded a little short even to his own ear. But, as far as Shayne was concerned, there was a damn good reason for his being annoyed.

He looked at the man sitting on his examining table. Precariously perched was more like it.

Shayne and Klondyke LeBlanc had been best friends since childhood, back when their schooling had meant sitting on the floor of Faye Elliot's drafty little cabin, listening to her read aloud as the wind whistled through the cracks. "Ike," as he was affectionately known, was one of the few people in that group, along with Ben and Shayne, who hadn't fled Alaska for one of the lower forty-nine as soon as he was of legal age.

Ike had bought into the Salty Saloon as soon as he'd scraped together enough money. Eventually he'd taken over and now he and his cousin, Jean Luc, ran it.

Neither Ike nor Jean Luc had ever known a sick day in their lives. Which was why, as Ike sat before him now, as healthy as a prize-winning stallion, Shayne had reason to question his presence.

A sheepish grin tugged on Ike's wide mouth. He avoided looking into Shayne's eyes. He'd never been very good at lying, something some viewed as a shortcoming in his line of work.

"Well, it's this cough, Shayne."

Ike tapped his chest for emphasis, then coughed, rather dramatically. In the middle of his performance, his brown eyes slanted toward the waiting room, hoping to catch another glimpse of the woman who had ushered him in so nicely. The door separating the two areas had accidentally been left standing slightly ajar when she'd walked out.

Shayne crossed his arms in front of him, not buying into this third-rate performance. "My guess is that it would be your knee that's giving you trouble."

That caught Ike's attention. Arched dark eyebrows drew together over a surprisingly aristocratic nose. "My knee?"

"Yes." Shayne pointed to the leg dangling over the side of the table that was closest to the door. "The one you're going to land on after you fall off the table if you keeping leaning over like that." Walking over to the door, Shayne shut it. "Why are you really here?" As if he didn't know.

"I told you, it's this cough—" The sheepish grin broadened. Knowing when he was caught, Ike surrendered the lie amiably. After all, he and Shayne had shared a drink or three in their time. Nothing bonded two men together more than that. "And to check out the new talent," Ike confessed.

Ike began to button up his shirt, the expression on his face distracted. Since the reason for his visit was out, there was no longer any need to behave like a patient.

"Haven't seen a woman that handsome around here since..." Slipping the ends of his shirt back into his jeans, he paused as he came to a realization. "I don't recall *ever* seeing a woman that handsome before." For a muscular man he moved with a certain easy grace. He eased himself off the table. "What's she doing here?"

"You tell me," Shayne suggested. "I'm sure the rumor mill is already grinding." It had probably started as soon as she'd set foot in Hades.

"It's grinding, all right, but I figured you'd be the one to know, since she's here with you."

Ike eyed him. "You send for her?" The fact would surprise him only because it was Shayne. Mail-order brides, or their modern equivalent, were not entirely unheard of in these parts. Ethan Parks had met his Emma that way and they seemed happy enough.

"No."

Shayne removed the stethoscope from his neck. He supposed that, in the absolute sense, this was a pleasant change from his usual hectic pace. Today, so far, no one'd had so much as a hangnail. Just terminal nosiness.

He could see that Ike was still waiting for him to elaborate. "Ben did."

Ike whistled softly between his teeth. "She's Ben's?" And then he scratched the back of his head. It didn't add up. "But he—"

"Ran off with Lila. Yes, I'm aware of that." Shayne thought of the note that was still in the pocket of his parka. "Painfully aware of that."

Ike's laugh, hearty and lusty, echoed in the office.

Shayne saw nothing funny in the situation. "Trust Ben to have two of them."

Shayne had no idea why that comment rankled him the way that it did. Or who he was taking offense for, Ben or Sydney. He just knew it annoyed him.

"He doesn't *have* two of them. He has Lila." Shayne nodded toward the outer office. "This one's just decided to stay on for a while, that's all."

That was good enough for Ike. He rubbed his hands together in anticipation. "Well, a while's all we're asking." He slipped on his fur-lined jacket, then set his black hat at a jaunty angle on his dark blond head. "What's her name, anyway?"

Shayne was surprised that wasn't common knowledge, too. "Sydney."

"Sydney?" Ike rolled the name around his tongue and made a face. "Damn silly name for a woman, especially a woman who looks like that, if you ask me."

"No one's asking you."

Hooded eyes scrutinized Shayne closely. "Hey, you're even testier than usual. Something bothering you?" A new light of understanding came into Ike's eyes. "You and her aren't—"

"No, we 'aren't,'" Shayne assured him quickly.

He had a pretty good idea he knew what Ike was implying. One hint, one ambiguous statement, and gossip would be off and running. In his experience, men were far worse than women.

"I just don't like having my time wasted by people who come here under false pretenses." He moved to the door and waited for Ike to join him. "The past three days, healthy, strapping men have been filing in here, mumbling things about bellyaches, flu, hair falling out— anything—just to come in and look her over."

If he was being admonished, Ike didn't seem to notice. "You get a box of candy delivered, Shayne, people are going to want to at least get a sniff of it." A wistful look came over his rugged face. "Chocolate's rare in these parts. Especially chocolate in a classy container."

Female companionship was always at a high premium in Hades. The mainstay of the town being the lumber mill, the workforce was almost all male. Except, of course, for the Widow Turner, who owned the mill and had buried three husbands. That made any woman who came into Hades fair and highly desirable game.

Shayne had often wondered, with such an eye for the ladies, why Ike hadn't left Alaska long ago. Or, if not Alaska, at least Hades.

He smiled tolerantly as he opened the door for Ike. "Try not to trip on your tongue on the way out."

Ike pretended to take offense, though he was too easygoing and good-natured to ever become annoyed.

"I'm not about to trip over anything—" And then an idea struck him. His eyes gleamed as he poked a finger into Shayne's chest. "Hey, you know what we should do?"

Shayne had no idea what Ike was thinking and even felt a little leery about asking. Not that he had to. Whether he asked or not, Ike would tell him.

"No, what?"

"Give her a party. A real big bash. Make her feel real welcome here." As soon as the words were out of his mouth, he started making plans. "Maybe then she'll stay permanently."

It was a bad notion all around. "I don't think—"

But Ike had already sold himself on the idea. He strode out into the waiting area and planted himself in front of Sydney's desk, his knuckles digging into the worn wood as he leaned toward her.

"Hey, darlin', how would you like to come to a party?"

She responded to both the wide grin on his face and the one in his voice. "A party?"

"Yeah." Ike glanced over his shoulder at Shayne as if backup was coming from that direction. "It's in your honor."

That took Sydney a minute to absorb. She glanced at Shayne, but nothing coming from that quarter enlightened her. "Mine?"

One of the men in the waiting room cheered his support of the idea.

Half the men in the room would have gladly supported any excuse for an extra round of beer, Shayne thought cynically. After a hard day at the mill, going to the Salty Saloon and knocking a few back with their friends was all some of the men had to look forward to.

"Sure. Hades is a real friendly place." Ike chuckled as he straightened. Man, but she smelled good. Someone should warn her about that. "Time you met some of your neighbors and such. What do you say? Six o'clock tonight?"

"Tonight?" When had all this been decided? Sydney wondered. Did Shayne have a hand in this? But looking at him, she knew without being told that he hadn't. He didn't seem like a man who fancied parties or noisy gatherings. "Aren't you moving a little fast?"

"Have to in these parts in order to keep warm," Ike said. The chuckle deepened into a lusty laugh. He winked at her, the dark brown brow wriggling. "Shayne knows the way, though he don't bend an elbow very much anymore," Ike imparted to her sorrowfully. "And if he don't bring you, darlin'," Ike announced gallantly, knowing he had to get his marker in early, "I'll come get you myself."

About to leave, Ike stopped long enough to look around the waiting room. It was filled to capacity with men, all of whom he had served over his stained counter at one time or another. Most far more than once. "You're all invited."

Cheers met his announcement.

And that, Ike figured, took care of the invitations. Turning around again, he pointed an index finger at Sydney, simulating an old-fashioned six-shooter about to be fired. "See you tonight, darlin'."

"He's very friendly," she said to Shayne as the outer door closed behind Ike. She had to admit, the impromptu invitation really made her feel welcomed here.

Shayne watched Ike through the window as the man trudged away. "That's one way to put it."

Curious, Sydney looked at him. "And how would you put it?"

"You don't want to know."

Shayne scanned the waiting room, taking a long, hard look at the remaining men. The ones who hadn't been lucky enough to secure a chair leaned against the wall or sat on the floor. There wasn't much walking space to be had.

Time to clear the area.

"All right, everybody, this is Sydney Elliot—no relation to Faye Elliot," Shayne qualified. "She's going to be staying on for a while as my assistant until she realizes that it's too damn cold here and moves on. If you want to see her, do it on your own time, not mine." He walked over to the front door and opened it. Cold air rushed in, chilling him, but he held the door wide open, waiting. "Now, I'd appreciate it if everyone who's not really sick leaves. I need the space for real patients."

A low rumble of dissatisfaction undulated through the crowd as men of all ages rose to their feet beside their standing comrades. Slowly, they trickled out the door.

Several extended greetings to Sydney as they filed out, promising to see her later tonight at the Salty. She noticed that their words evoked an even darker frown from Shayne.

She waited until everyone had left and Shayne had closed the door again. The waiting room was empty. "I know this is your clinic, but you could have worded that a little more politely."

He didn't take criticism well, constructive or otherwise. Besides, where did she get off telling him how to behave around people he'd known far longer than he'd known her?

"I know those men. Being polite wouldn't have gotten me anywhere with them. You have to haul them out like mules."

"If you say so." The image left something to be desired. "By the way, you were wrong."

Was she determined to argue about this? "I already said there's only one way to—"

She shook her head, stopping him before he could continue. "No, I mean about my not being related to Faye Elliot."

That took him by surprise. As far as he knew, Faye Elliot had never mentioned anything about having a family, only her father, and Reverend Elliot had died long before Shayne had been born.

"You're related to Miss Faye?"

Sydney nodded. "She was my father's aunt. He used to get postcards from her occasionally." She could remember how excited she'd get each time one arrived. The scenes depicted on them had looked so exotic to her. A fond smile curved her mouth. "I kept them all in a scrapbook. Sometimes there were letters." Long, voluminous letters—filled with details of daily life in a harsh, unforgiving land—that arrived sporadically, coming every few years just when it seemed that Aunt Faye had forgotten about them.

"I always envisioned her as this brave pioneer woman, carving out a life for herself after her father passed away."

In the tradition of a pioneer, Aunt Faye had come to Alaska with her father, an ordained minister, to do work among the Inuits. She'd often written that, rather than save their souls the way he'd intended, her father said that they had saved his by renewing his zest for life.

Shayne leaned a hip against the reception desk, looking at Sydney and trying to detect a resemblance between her and the small, stately woman who had taught him how to read and write and told long, beautiful stories about far-off, exotic places.

Maybe around the mouth, he thought. He could remember the way Miss Faye would set her mouth when she was attempting to coax a pupil into giving the right answer to a question. Pure determination. Rather like the way Sydney had looked at the airport.

"Folks said her father died trying to get to a sick child in the village." Bemused, amazed, Shayne shook his head, looking at Sydney again. "You're related to Miss Faye."

She smiled, amused at the expression on his face. He looked as if someone had just told him that the answer to two plus two was secretly five. "That's what I said."

"She was my teacher. My first teacher," he amended.

And one of the kindest people he had ever met. But he never recalled seeing her smile. She always struck him as a woman who lived with some deep sorrow.

"Small world."

And getting smaller all the time, he thought. "Listen, perhaps later you might like to—"

The front door banged open, blotting out whatever he was going to say and snaring their attention.

A towering man rushed in, a half-crazed look on his face. In his arms was a screaming child of no more than five. Blood smeared the man's face and clothing. It took Sydney a moment to pinpoint the source. The boy's left hand was wrapped in a towel—a very blood-soaked towel. Shayne moved from her side and took the boy into his arms.

The boy's pitiful cries of pain ricocheted around the room.

"Doctor, it's his hand, his finger." Hysteria built in the man's deep voice, matching the volume the child was achieving. "Oh God, I told him not to touch it."

Shayne raised his voice to be heard above both of them. "What happened?" he demanded.

"I don't know!" the man practically wailed, shadowing Shayne as he turned to enter the examining room. "One minute he was playing with his friends, showing them my fishing equipment, and then suddenly, I heard him screaming and there was blood everywhere."

Sydney positioned herself between the man and Shayne, placing her hands on the man's trembling, blood-stained arms. He would only get in Shayne's way.

"It's going to be all right," she said soothingly. "Just wait here, please." She blocked his access to the inner room. "You won't do him any good in here."

"But he's my son."

She met the angered look head-on. "No one's disputing that. And if you want your son to get the best care as quickly as possible, you're going to have to stay out here."

For a second she thought the man would toss her aside, out of his way. And then a hopeless look entered his eyes. Hopeless because he knew there was nothing he could do.

"But my boy…he needs me." The words were shrouded in despair.

"He needs to calm down more." She backstepped toward the door, watching, to make sure he wouldn't follow. "We can handle this." It was a promise she had no authority to make.

Turning on her heel, she hurried into the room, shutting the door behind her. Quickly, she pulled out a fresh covering for the examining table.

"The instruments—" Shayne began as he placed the boy on the table.

"Got 'em," she announced, sliding the tray parallel to the table.

The boy's screams rose in intensity as a new fear compounded his pain. He jerked upright the moment his back came in contact with the table. Sydney grasped the boy's right hand and wrapped her fingers around the small wrist.

"Look at me," she urged softly. His head tossing from side to side, Sidney knew they had to get him to lie still for the injection. She raised her eyes to Shayne. "What's his name?"

"Joseph," Shayne answered as he tore open a fresh package of surgical gloves on the tray and pulled them on.

"Joseph. Look at me," she ordered, her voice soft,

commanding. When the boy didn't comply, she turned his head toward her with her free hand, forcing him to look in her direction. "It's going to be all right. Do you hear me? Dr. Shayne is going to help you feel better. You're going to be all right. I promise."

Her eyes met Shayne's. She could see admonishment in them.

"I promise," she repeated. The boy needed to hear that more than he needed to be apprised of the possibilities that faced him.

She could see Joseph's heart pounding in his chest as he cringed at the sight of the needle Shayne was preparing. "No, no, don't hurt me. Please don't hurt me. It hurts. It hurts…it hurts," he sobbed.

Her own heart was in her mouth. She'd been around cuts and bruises, but nothing approaching the apparent severity of this young child's injury.

Releasing her grasp on his wrist, Sydney threaded her fingers through Joseph's and held on tight, trying to fuse courage into his small body. "Of course it hurts. You had a very big accident." She talked quickly, hoping to distract him long enough for Shayne to administer the anesthetic.

"And there's going to be a great scar—something to impress your friends with. But first you have to stop screaming and let the doctor do his work."

Huge tears rolled down Joseph's cheeks as he winced and tried to focus on her.

"Dr. Shayne's going to sew up your hand so you can play again. But he needs your help to do it, okay?"

His tears continued to flow, but slowly, the terror receded and he began to calm down. Within a few minutes, the anesthetic Shayne had given him began to take effect. Joseph's eyes drooped as he became drowsy.

Throughout it all, Sydney never stopped talking to him. She continued, touching on everything she could think of that might interest a boy, until the surgery was finally over.

Sydney didn't feel as if she released the breath she was holding until an eternity later when Shayne placed a groggy, bandaged Joseph into his father's outstretched arms.

He slipped a comforting arm around the man's shoulders. "There shouldn't be any permanent damage. You got him here in time."

Larry Elder hugged his son to him.

"I want you to give him two of these for the pain every four hours the first day." Shayne unlocked the small cabinet by his desk and doled out eight white pills into an envelope. Very carefully, he sealed it. "After that, it should be all right."

He tucked the pills into the man's shirt pocket, then tugged the open jacket back into place. "If not, I want to see him. Any sort of problem, I want to see him. Otherwise, bring him by in four days, I'll change the bandages and check on my handiwork." He walked over to the front door and opened it for them.

Larry Elder nodded his dark head at each instruction. "Right, absolutely. And thanks again." His dark eyes filled with tears. "Really."

Shayne spared them both. "That's what I'm here for. And next time, lock up your fishing equipment," he added.

He shut the door behind Elder. That was the last of the codeine pills, he thought. He would have to take a run down to the hospital pharmacy in Anchorage to get more.

When he turned around, Sydney was looking at him. "Nice job."

He shrugged off the compliment. He was a doctor, he was supposed to be equal to these kinds of situations. "Thanks." Shayne nodded, realizing she hadn't lost her head the way his last assistant had. Whether by instinct or design, Sydney Elliot seemed to know her way around an emergency. Maybe that story about wanting to be a doctor had been on the level. "I guess I could say the same to you."

She wondered if he felt as reluctant as he sounded. "If you want to."

She knew how to draw things out of a person, Shayne thought grudgingly. "All right, I want to. You did a good job, especially calming the boy down. You're right, kids do like you."

She smiled. "Most adults do, too."

He thought of the men who had been in earlier. "I noticed." He dragged a hand through his hair, feeling drained now that the crisis was over. "So, I take it you want to go to that thing tonight at the Salty?"

Sydney was surprised he even had to ask. But then again, he would. "Wouldn't be right not to, seeing as how I'm supposed to be the guest of honor." She peered at his face. "Will you come with me?"

He shrugged again. "I suppose I'll have to. The place is going to be full of men, falling all over each other just to get close to you. Someone has to protect you from that."

So he was going to be her reluctant knight, was he? She rather liked the sound of that. But she didn't want him to think she was some helpless little female who needed looking after. It'd been a very long time since she'd been helpless.

"I can take care of myself."

He was beginning to believe that. Still, she was under his roof and his responsibility. "I'll come along anyway."

She smiled at him. "I'd like that."

She might, he mused, but the problem was, he wasn't too sure if he would.

Or worse, that he would.

Chapter Eight

Shayne didn't like the way Jean Luc was looking at Sydney. As if she were a rack of freshly roasted lamb and he was a timber wolf just coming off a fourteen-day hunger strike. Hell, if he were being honest with himself, Shayne'd have to say that he didn't particularly like the way any of the men crowding into the seventy-five-year-old saloon were looking at her.

One of the McGregor twins bumped into Shayne as he tried to forge his way into the thick of things. Into the huge misshapen circle of men weaving in and around Sydney. Every damn one of them wanted to get close to her. Like seals nudging each other out of the way for the best sunning place on the rock.

She was the only woman in the place. Not an unusual fact on its own, but a source of growing irritation for him right now.

Sydney looked as though she were enjoying all this

shallow attention she was receiving. She wasn't flirting the way he'd seen Ben's Lila do, but then, the last time he'd seen the woman who'd made his brother lose what little sense he had, it'd been several years ago. She'd been just a slip of a girl then, testing her powers, seeing how far they'd take her.

This was no mere girl at the opposite end of the Salty. Sydney was a woman full-blown and ripe. So ripe, she could make a grown man ache just by being there.

Shayne's fingers tightened around the handle of his mug. Sydney had no need to test any of her powers. He figured she knew what they were.

A jukebox, stocked with songs from a decade or two ago, was vainly trying to pierce the din of raised voices and laughter within the wide, wood-paneled building that had been painstakingly remodeled to resemble Juneau's Red Dog Saloon.

It hardly scratched the surface.

It seemed odd to Shayne, with all the noise that was ricocheting about in the Salty, that he could hear her laughter above everything else. It wasn't loud, or high, just haunting.

Like the scent she wore.

Like the look in her eyes.

He raised the mug to his lips, then put it down again, forgetting to drink as he watched Nils O'Hara whisper something in Sydney's ear. She laughed in response, the sound piercing him. Something stirred inside Shayne. He hadn't a clue as to what. The closest he could place it was the way it felt when he'd once gotten himself lost in the deserted mine for more than two days. His stomach was so empty and pinched so bad it felt as if it'd been stapled to his back.

It felt kind of like that. Only worse.

He frowned into his drink. It was none of his business, of course, what she did or didn't do. None at all. Still, he didn't have to like it.

And he didn't.

"Remind me to thank your brother the next time I see him." Shayne looked up to find Ike across from him at the bar.

Ike was wiping at an imaginary stain. Ike was always massaging the wood, polishing it when there was a lull in business, pampering it like an obsequious lover in between pouring drinks when business was booming. He loved this old place and it showed.

Leaning one elbow on the bar, Shayne looked down at the amber liquid in his glass mug. The overhead light grazed it, dancing along the surface like a fairy trying to pick her way over tiny stones in a rushing brook. He stared at it for a long moment before looking up again.

"What do you want to thank him for?" It took an effort not to growl the question. He was having a hell of a time holding on to his temper tonight, something that usually gave him no trouble at all.

Ike laughed. "Last time I remember business being this good, a blizzard trapped a quarter of the mill workers in here. They drank for the duration. Almost drank me dry." The till had overflowed that time, Ike recalled fondly. "When the weather finally let up, they were feeling no pain." The look on his face was almost sentimental as he remembered. "Jean Luc and I had to drive them all home, but hell, it was worth it. That's when I got the money to buy the jukebox and the satellite dish."

Half the time the television set had as much snow on the screen as they had outside. Shayne looked at Ike's grinning face. "Yeah, well, glad you're so happy."

Jean Luc was busy tending the other end of the bar.

Ike figured he could pick up the overflow for a few minutes. He stopped rubbing the counter and leaned forward to peer at Shayne's face, growing serious.

"What's eating at you? Times tough without Ben?"

The last thing Shayne wanted to do was discuss his frame of mind. He didn't believe in baring his soul, not even to someone who'd known him for years. "You might say that."

"Heard from him, yet?"

"No, not yet."

Not that he expected to. It'd been less than a week since Ben and Lila had taken off. Ben was undoubtedly high on his newly achieved status as husband. Or fool. More than likely, knowing Ben, he'd be like that for some time to come. Once he came down, Ben might think to call him, but Shayne wasn't about to hold his breath until that happened.

"Look at it this way, you get to keep what he left behind." With a lift of a brow, he indicated where Sydney was standing with a nod of his head.

Ike had survived all that Alaska had to throw at a man, partially because he'd always been able to see the bright side of everything. His sense of hope was also what made him perfect for his chosen vocation.

Shayne looked at him sharply. "She's a woman, Ike, not a shirt."

Ike looked thoughtfully over toward where Sydney was holding court. He watched the way she held herself, the way she moved when she turned to look at someone. Made a man start thinking about giving up the high life and settling down.

"Sure wouldn't mind keeping her," Ike murmured, appreciation throbbing in his voice. And then he saw the look in Shayne's eyes. It was the kind of look that made a man step out of range. He'd seen that kind of look before. It had possession written all over it. Well, well, who would have thought it? "You're going to have to make up your mind about this, Shayne."

Shayne's expression darkened. What the hell was Ike going on about now? "About what?"

Ike took no heed of the warning note in his friend's voice. He'd never been afraid to talk to Shayne, not even when Shayne's wife had picked up and left him. Everyone else in town had avoided the subject with Shayne because they were afraid of having their heads bitten off.

Ike looked Shayne in the eye. "Either you don't want her, or you do."

What the hell made Ike think he had the slightest interest in the woman? "You've been sampling too much of your stock, Ike. I already said—"

"I know what you *said*," Ike stated flatly. "How you look when you're saying it is a whole different matter." Because Shayne didn't immediately jump down his throat, Ike went a little further. "I think she makes you remember that you're a flesh-and-blood man and not just the local witch doctor."

That was so absurd, Shayne didn't know where to begin to refute Ike's observation. Exasperated, Shayne waved a disgusted hand at him. "You don't know what you're talking about."

Ike's broad shoulders rumbled beneath his shirt as they rose and fell, not in surrender but in momentary retreat. "Have it your way." He looked at Shayne's mug, the contents of which had hardly changed since he'd first poured it. "Are you going to drink that or just pray over it like you've been doing for the past two hours?"

From the corner of his eye, Shayne noticed a man

three stools over raise his hand, trying to get Ike's attention. Shayne pointed toward him. "Go peddle your spirits, Ike. Someone's buying. I'm doing fine just the way I am."

Shayne could have sworn he heard Ike mumble, "Your opinion," as he moved away to see what the man would have. Shayne wasn't about to ask Ike to repeat what he'd said. Ike just might tell him, and he was in no mood for more lectures.

Eyeing the contents of his mug, he finally raised it to his lips and took a long swallow. The beer tasted particularly bitter tonight.

He glanced toward Sydney again. There was a fresh circle of lechers around her.

Or maybe that was just the taste in his mouth and not the beer, he thought. No reason for the latter.

It didn't change anything, though.

Someone jostled against him, this time trying to get to the bathroom. Shayne was surprised there wasn't a huge line snaking its way out of the tiny accommodation. Ike had recently opened up a fresh keg, the third one tonight.

Ike was right, he mused. There was an inordinate amount of people in here. Far more than he ever remembered seeing. Hades's population hovered around five hundred souls at any given time. Right now, it felt as if two-thirds of them had shoehorned their way inside the 24 by 48 building.

The press of bodies was getting to be more than he could put up with. It was decidedly hot in here and growing more so. He'd removed his parka over an hour ago but that was no longer good enough. He needed to get some air, even if it was freezing outside. It'd be an improvement, if only for a few minutes.

Making up his mind, Shayne plucked his parka from one of the hooks that lined the back wall and began the slow journey toward the front door. He felt like a salmon trying to make it upstream. A salmon encountering a lot of other salmon swimming in the opposite direction.

He hadn't been out of her line of vision all evening, no matter who had been in front of her or what they'd been saying. Sydney thought of Shayne as her anchor. She saw him now, making his way to the door, despite the fact that she was carrying on a seven-way conversation with the Riley brothers and their cousins, a collection of men, mill workers all, ranging from the age of eighteen to seventy-one.

Shayne was leaving. The thought telegraphed itself through her brain. Was he going home without her? She wouldn't put it past him. Shayne was too accustomed to keeping his own counsel to probably even remember that he'd brought her here. There was no way she was about to be abandoned again. Twice in one week was twice too many.

"Excuse me," she murmured to the man directly in her path. She tried to move around him, but it wasn't as easy as she would have liked.

The youngest Riley, who fancied himself more of a ladies' man, was reluctant to let her get away. "Are you leaving?"

"Don't go yet," someone said from behind her. "It's still early."

She was already halfway to the door. Glancing over her shoulder, amusement played over her generous mouth. "How can you tell?"

The question was met with more than slightly inebriated laughter. The sound, swelling and lusty, followed her as the crowd obligingly parted the way it hadn't for Shayne.

The blast of cold air that met her as she walked out the front door of the Salty instantly stung her cheeks. It was like stepping into a cold shower, only far worse. The warm cocoon that had surrounded her only a moment ago cracked wide open and fell off.

Shivering, she pulled her parka closer to her, overlapping the two ends. In her haste to get out, she hadn't bothered to zip it up. Worse, she realized belatedly, she must have dropped her gloves inside somewhere. They weren't in her pockets.

Shayne turned when he heard the volley of voices crescendo then ebb as the door opened and closed. He raised a brow, surprised that she'd followed him.

"Had enough fawning?"

The choice of words confused her. "'Fawning'?"

"Fawning," he repeated. When she continued to look at him as if he were making things up, he elaborated. "Falling all over themselves to get close to you. Have you had enough of it?"

He looked angry. She had no doubt that somehow in his mind, it had to be her fault. Now what had she done?

"'Enough'? I wasn't aware that I was trying to get my fill." She shivered as the wind found its way under her parka. Why did he have to take such a dour view of things? He certainly wasn't a thing like his brother. But then, Ben was gone and Shayne was here. And he'd offered her a place to stay and a job. That counted for something. Her expression softened. "They were just being friendly."

Friendly, hell, Shayne muttered to himself. Was that what it was called these days? He laughed shortly. "Any friendlier and you'd all be bedding down together for the night.''

She stiffened and raised her chin, her eyes narrowing. She'd just about had her fill of the Doctors Kerrigan, present and absent. This one refused to react to kindness. ''Is there something you'd like to say to me in a straightforward manner, Shayne?''

He looked away. By his estimation, he'd already said too much. ''No.''

Sydney wasn't about to drop the subject that readily. ''I forgot, you don't like to say too much at all. But that doesn't stop you from thinking it, does it?''

His expression was mild when he looked at her again, his words carefully measured. Like the calculated steps involved in assembling a bomb. ''Last time I noticed, a man was still entitled to his own thoughts.''

She'd been having a good time, a harmless good time. She didn't think that was too much to ask, given what she'd been put through by the thoughtless actions of his brother. What was it that Shayne wanted from her? Why was he condemning her?

''Maybe, but when they're written all over your face, then I'd like to hear them.''

His eyes met hers. There was fire in them. A fire so intense, Shayne felt as if he could warm himself in them. Burn himself. ''If they're all over my face then you already know what they are.''

The man was insufferable and infuriating. ''Did you take a vow of semisilence or something?'' She could feel her temper flaring. ''You are the most difficult man to get a straight answer out of that I've ever met.''

Her eyes were beautiful, Shayne thought. Even in the dim light coming from the saloon. He could feel himself becoming hypnotized. He struggled to keep from going under.

"I give very straight answers, Sydney. And I don't lie. Be very sure you want to hear what I have to say before you ask."

He was putting her on notice. She wrapped her arms around herself, tucking her hands against her body. Her fingers were growing numb. "You don't like me very much, do you?"

Shayne didn't want it to sound personal. Personal carried implications with it that he wasn't ready to deal with. "I have nothing against you."

That, Sydney realized, left only one conclusion to be drawn. "Then it's the gender you don't care for?"

"I have no feelings for the 'gender' one way or another." At least, that was the way he was trying to keep it. But dealing with this particular member of the opposite sex threw a serious crimp into his resolve. "Unlike those men in there—" he nodded toward the building behind her "—I'm not in the market for anything— no night of hot love, no lifetime of companionship. I just don't like to see people make fools of themselves, that's all."

She didn't want to take that as an insult, but what else could he mean? And where did he get off, judging her? Sydney's eyes narrowed. "Are you referring to me or to the men?"

The heat that had assaulted him inside the saloon and had driven him out, seeking relief, had completely dissipated. If he was cold, Shayne thought, she had to be colder. She was standing with her parka unzipped and her hands had no gloves on them. Fool woman must have left her brains parked in there with those fawning jackasses. She was going to get sick and then he'd have one more patient to add to his roster. Just what he wanted.

"Both." Frowning a silent reprimand, Shayne stepped toward her, took the two ends of her parka and hooked one into the other. With a snap of his wrist, he moved the zipper all the way up. "Where are your gloves?"

He was talking to her as if she was younger than Sara. It killed her to admit that she didn't know. "I seem to have lost them."

Shaking his head, he stripped off his gloves and held them out to her. "Here."

They were far too big for her. "I can't take your gloves."

She'd hardly finished the protest before he was tugging the gloves on her hands himself. "If you're going to work for me, I don't want you starting out by taking sick time."

Sydney shook her head, amused and oddly disappointed at the same time. This could have been a very tender scene if he hadn't sounded like an irate employer. Still, her mouth curved at the humor of it. "You have a way of ruining a moment, you know that?"

Women definitely came from another planet. He hadn't the slightest idea what she was talking about. "We weren't having a 'moment.'"

But even as he said the words, that strange restlessness returned, a little stronger, a little more disorienting. Instead of moving to his car, he found himself just standing there, looking at her. Looking into her eyes.

She trapped him there, he realized too late. No matter how much he struggled, he couldn't seem to free himself. He just kept falling. Deeper. Losing his train of thought.

Losing himself.

"A word of advice," he said, striving to think rationally. "Stop wearing that scent. Bears are attracted to perfume and cologne. Draws them out."

"I'm not wearing perfume. Or cologne."

Then that scent, he groaned, had to be her.

The restlessness gave way to an impulse that spun out of nowhere and refused to retreat. Doggedly, it ensnared him, taking hold and urging him on.

He hadn't had enough ale to inebriate a hamster, Shayne reasoned, so he couldn't blame his next move on what he'd consumed.

He blamed it on being male. There was nothing else left to buffer him from his actions. There had to be some reason, some explanation, why one minute he was shoving his gloves onto her hands and the next he was holding her. Holding her and on the verge of doing something he knew he would regret all through this long, lonely Alaskan night.

He did it anyway.

Pulses throbbing in his temples, he lowered his mouth and kissed her. Maybe to find out what it was like. Maybe just to still his curiosity.

Maybe because he'd finally lost his mind. A man had no business standing in near-freezing weather, kissing a woman when he had no gloves on.

This was the last thing she'd expected—and the first thing she'd wanted, Sydney realized with a start as everything that had gone into a deep freeze suddenly thawed within her. There were a thousand reasons why she might kiss someone.

And only one why she kissed him.

But right now Sydney wasn't thinking of reasons or explanations. She wasn't thinking at all. She wasn't doing anything except kissing—and feeling. And maybe hanging on for dear life as the bottom dropped out from beneath her feet.

Shayne's arms tightened around her as he pulled Sydney closer. He could feel the effect of her kiss throughout his whole body.

He'd been kicked by a mule once. The animal's hoof had just grazed his shoulder, but for weeks after, he'd imagined what the full impact might have felt like. He'd never have to wonder anymore. He knew.

But with a mule, he wouldn't have gone back for more. He did now. His mouth slanted over hers again and again. Each time, a little more forcefully. Each time, yielding a little piece of himself until it felt as if there was hardly anything left of him. Hardly anything to anchor him to the world.

The realization that he might plummet over the edge had him pulling up sharply.

Sydney, feeling more dazed than she had when she'd first woken up this morning, tried to focus on him. "Was *that* a moment?"

"What?" Shayne tried to make sense of the words, then remembered what she'd said earlier. "Oh. Maybe."

Why did she have to ask questions, questions that spawned questions within his own brain? He didn't want questions, he wanted answers. Such as the one addressing why he had just done that.

Backing away from her as if she'd suddenly turned into a live electrical wire, Shayne tried to collect his scattered thoughts. Only scraps came within reach.

"Are you ready to go home, yet?"

Sydney didn't know what she was ready for, only that she might have made one of the biggest blunders of her life. She knew she wasn't ready for this, wasn't ready to be with anyone. Wasn't ready to even be kissed by anyone, really. Except that she had been. And more than that, she'd kissed back.

Now what?

He was looking at her, waiting for an answer. She pressed her lips together.

"Sure." He took her arm, to lead her to his car. A light dusting of snow began to fall as she looked back at the saloon. "Shouldn't I say something to someone in there, let them know I'm leaving?" It didn't seem right just to pick up and go without a word.

Shayne had no intention of letting her go back inside. If she did, there was no telling how long it would take to get her out again.

"Don't worry, they'll figure it out on their own," he assured her.

The snow was coming down harder. There was always a chance the weather would turn ugly, and he wanted to make it home before that happened. He didn't like the idea of leaving his children alone for the night, even if Asia was there with them. It wasn't the same as being there with them himself.

"I've got to be up early tomorrow. But you can sleep in." Unlocking the car doors, he opened hers and then rounded the hood to his side.

She looked at him over the hood, blinking back snow-flakes as they landed on her lashes. "Firing me already?"

From where he stood, she looked like someone out of an old-fashioned melodrama, flirting with him. He should have been laughing at the thought, not allowing it to curl through his belly like hot cereal on a cold morning. He squelched the desire to taste snowflakes as they melted along her eyelids.

Instead, he got into the vehicle. "No, I've got to fly

to Anchorage tomorrow morning to get more codeine pills.'' Weather permitting, he added silently. ''Joseph got the last of my supply.''

And Shayne hadn't charged his father for the medication, Sydney remembered. He was more the good doctor than he wanted to let on. ''Can I come with you?''

''Why?'' He glanced at her suspiciously as he turned on the ignition. ''I thought flying made you nervous.''

''That's why.'' Sydney could see he thought she was crazy. ''I don't want to be nervous,'' she explained. ''I want to be able to conquer every fear.'' She refused to be held a prisoner by feelings, *any* feelings. ''If I'm going to stay here, maybe I should learn how to fly a plane.''

I wouldn't want to be on that flight, Shayne quipped to himself as he pulled out of the parking lot. ''You can't do that from the passenger side.''

''No, but I can in the pilot's seat.'' She half turned in her seat, looking at him. Even sitting so close, she couldn't make out his expression. But she could guess. ''You could teach me.''

Shayne was glad there was nothing on the road ahead of him. The request wasn't one he'd been prepared for.

''I could also grow feathers and fly. Neither one is likely to happen in the foreseeable future.''

Like Mac, Sydney conceded, Shayne was going to require a lot of work. ''You don't make it easy for anyone to get along with you, do you?''

Shayne saw no reason to take exception to something he knew was true. In this case, he was trying not to be accommodating.

''Nope.''

He was going to be a *real* challenge. But not one, she

decided, running the tip of her tongue along her lower lip and tasting him, that she wasn't up to.

Turning her face toward him, she smiled serenely.

Though he couldn't pinpoint exactly why, Shayne had the uneasy feeling he'd silently been put on notice.

Chapter Nine

Shayne guided his plane past the only cloud formation around for miles. It was as white and pristine as the snow below.

The winds were with him for a change, and he was making good time. Not that he generally liked to hurry his flights. Flying was the only time he got to really relax. There were no demands on him here; no one who needed him immediately. Up here, with nothing but the sky wrapped around him and the earth below, he was able to let his mind occupy a timeless space where there were no problems for him to deal with.

Except this time, the problem had hitched a ride with him.

Again.

He glanced to his right. Sydney was sitting in the seat next to him, just the way she had on the half dozen or so other medical supply runs he'd made since she'd wangled her first flight with him several weeks ago. He still wasn't completely sure how she'd managed to talk him into it. Into coming along with him when he valued his privacy more than a miner valued his first panful of gold.

He'd kissed his privacy goodbye the first time he allowed her to step into his plane.

Even if she hadn't said a word, Shayne conceded, she would have filled the cockpit with just her presence. Just by being there, she seemed to disrupt the very air around her. Not to mention *him*.

"Disruptive" didn't begin to describe his train of thought, which derailed every time he came in contact with her.

But she wasn't not saying a word. She was saying a hell of a lot of them. No doubt about it, she'd come a long way since the first couple of flights when she'd sat quietly, obviously trying to regulate the pounding of her heart. Now, apparently having come to grips with her fear of flying in the small plane just the way she'd said she would, Sydney used their flight time to attempt to wear him down. She was as determined to get him to teach her how to fly as he was determined not to.

If the past few weeks was any indication, it was obvious she believed that if she talked long enough and hard enough, he would eventually give in.

As if he'd ever let her get her hands on his Cessna.

Still, it astounded Shayne that the woman just wouldn't give up, no matter how much he ignored her or turned her down. "Surrender" just wasn't in her vocabulary. Neither was quitting.

Sydney leaned forward to watch a flock of geese vanish into the horizon. It never ceased to astound her how each bird instinctively knew its position within the formation. She was still trying to find hers in the scheme of things. Although, she had a feeling, the move to Hades promised to bring her closer to that place.

She turned to look at Shayne's rigid profile. She certainly wasn't any closer to wearing him down. But that only made her more determined. There was only one other pilot in the area now that Ben wasn't around. But Jeb Kellogg was kept far too busy to take time to give her lessons. That left Shayne, who was as stubborn as a summer's day in Hades was long.

He'd only looked at her stonily when she'd offered to pay him for lessons. At the moment, he couldn't be cajoled or bought, but she intended to keep on trying one way or another until he agreed.

"I'm sure I'd be good at it if you just give me a chance."

Shayne should have known better than to think the lull in the conversation meant she'd given up. He kept his eyes straight ahead, even though he had to admit that she presented the more pleasing view.

"It's not like driving a car." How many ways and times had he said that already? She just couldn't seem to get it through her thick head. "You miscalculate here and there's no walking away from your mistake. It's a long first step down, Sydney."

The warning left her unfazed, just as all the other blatant warnings had. She was too positive a person to entertain the negative side of a situation for more than a moment.

"I won't be taking it." She stared at him, willing Shayne to look at her. "I'll have an excellent teacher who'll prepare me for any contingency."

He laughed to himself, shaking his head. Served him right for letting her come along with him. He'd known that this would be the topic of conversation. Why had he agreed?

The answer occurred to him, but he left it unexplored. It was better that way.

"Flattery isn't going to get you anywhere," he told her.

There was a pause before Sydney asked, "Then what will?"

It was an innocent enough question. Still, it seemed to almost pour along his skin, rousing a response that was formed completely against his will.

He kept the thought to himself. Thoughts like that could only lead to trouble for everyone, especially him. Once hinted at, there'd be no going back, and for now he didn't want to rock the boat. Against all his expectations, Sydney was working out surprisingly well at the clinic, not to mention the fact that she'd taken it upon herself to supplement whatever lessons Mrs. Kellogg taught the children. Even Mac seemed to look forward to doing homework at night. She certainly wasn't the liability he'd first thought she would be.

Not that, he amended quickly, her remaining involved at the clinic or with his children was by any means anything he was counting on permanently. But for now, it was going well.

If at times the sound of her voice as she read to Sara stirred him and led his mind onto paths best left untraveled, well, that was something he could deal with without letting anyone else know about it.

Least of all, the source of those fantasies.

He heard her draw a long breath. The woman was refueling. He knew he was in for another barrage of words. Sydney talked when he answered; she talked when he didn't. There didn't seem to be a way out for him, but he didn't want to continue going around and around about the lessons today.

In an effort to change the subject, Shayne pointed to a small dot on the pristine landscape that three snowstorms, one following on the heels of another, had recently created. He hadn't realized that they were this far south.

"That's Miss Faye's cabin down there, if you're interested." He knew that she would be. Sydney seemed to be interested in absolutely everything, no matter how trivial, and this, after all, had belonged to someone in her family. Or so she'd said.

Sydney immediately tried to see where he was pointing. She craned her neck for a better view. It was a single, lonely brown spot on the white terrain. One of the walls looked as if it was crumbling.

"That's where she lived?"

Shayne nodded. "For forty years, they say." He could only attest to the last eighteen of them.

The little cabin immediately captured her interest. She'd been meaning to ask if Aunt Faye's house was still standing, but so much else had been happening while she'd been trying to carve out a life here, she'd forgotten all about it.

"Is anyone living there now?" Sydney saw no signs of life in the area, but she'd learned that didn't mean anything up here. Still, it didn't appear as if there were any prints leading to or from the cabin. And if someone was living there, wouldn't they have fixed the wall?

In a moment, the cabin was far behind them.

"No, it's been deserted since she died." No one had been interested in appropriating the cabin. It was off the beaten path, even for out here.

It had looked so tiny, so fragile, from this vantage

point. A little, Shayne thought, like the photographs of Aunt Faye herself.

Sidney turned from the window. "Will you take me to see it?"

Habit had him starting to beg off, but then he shrugged. It might be interesting, at that, to see the old place again. He hadn't been within those four walls for almost fifteen years. He supposed a side trip might fit into his schedule somehow. Lately, he had a little more time on his hands than normal. That was Sydney's doing. She'd swiftly absorbed every aspect of running the clinic—except for the actual doctoring.

Not that she hadn't tried to do even that, a time or two. Just minor things, like chest colds and cuts, which she felt she was qualified to handle. The woman, given half a chance, was into everything.

Not for the first time, he thought that she would have been just what his brother needed to settle him into the stream of things.

His shrug was noncommittal. "When I get a chance."

She saw a chance to needle him a little and push her cause. "Of course, if I knew how to fly, I wouldn't have to bother you."

That made him laugh, really laugh. "Knowing you were up in the air with my plane would bother me a whole lot more than taking you would."

She rolled the sentence over in her mind. Amusement rose in her eyes as she asked, "Should I be flattered or insulted?"

That restlessness he was having such trouble shaking permanently was back, nibbling away at him. He knew it came with her presence. Which made his reasons for taking her with him a complete mystery.

"What you should be, is quiet," Shayne told her.

though his tone lacked conviction. "But I don't suppose there's much chance of that happening, is there?"

Sydney merely smiled.

The door groaned in protest as it was opened and Sara shrank back, grasping Sydney's hand. Even with mittens in the way, holding on to Sydney comforted her. Her father and brother had come with them, but it was Sydney on whom she relied to chase away her uncertainties. Sydney who understood why she was afraid in the first place.

"It's just a cabin, sugar," Sydney whispered, sensing her unease. "A tired, sad little cabin."

Sidney looked around. There was dirt, debris, and what looked to be broken furniture scattered within the cabin. Half the stairs leading to a loft were missing and the wind whistled through the gaping opening where part of the wall had collapsed.

It was hard picturing her great-aunt living here. Her letters had been so articulate, so alive. The day-to-day existence Aunt Faye had known was now all but buried beneath layers of cobwebbed dust. Sydney hadn't thought of spiders being this far north. She moved around slowly, trying to recreate a time in her mind when all this had been new. Trying to see it as it had been for Aunt Faye.

Sydney paused to right an overturned chair, only to have it fall again because one of the legs had rotted clear through. When it collapsed, Sara stifled a scream.

"Baby," Mac jeered, then cast a sidelong glance at his father, waiting for the reprimand.

"I am not," Sara denied, though she was clinging to Sydney when she said it.

"No, of course you're not," Sydney said softly. "It's natural to be a little spooked in a place like this."

"Spooks?" It was Mac's turn to look around with wide, uncertain eyes.

"Poor choice of words," Sydney apologized.

"And you used to come here to learn stuff?" Sara asked in hushed disbelief, turning toward Shayne.

Shayne was standing in front of the dormant fireplace, remembering. This was where he'd sat, looking into the dancing flames while Miss Faye read to them, or told them about some distant land that might as well have been on the far side of the moon for all the difference it had made to him at the time.

But he'd loved listening to her voice, to the cadence in it.

The cabin had seemed so much larger then, Shayne thought. He was almost sorry that he'd come. Memories belonged in the past, untouched.

He turned from the fireplace. "Every day until I was old enough to go to school in Shelbyville."

Shayne glanced toward Mac, who was picking at something in the corner with a stick. Sydney'd been the one to suggest that bringing Mac and Sara along would make for a good family outing. He hadn't been convinced of the wisdom of it, but Sara had been eager. Mac, who had wanted no part of it, had ridden, silent and surly, in the back of the plane. He wasn't so surly now.

Shayne crossed to him. "What'd you find?"

Mac picked up a faded, torn photograph of a woman standing in front of the cabin. He held it up for his father's inspection. "Just this."

Taking it, Shayne brushed aside the thick layers of dust with his fingertips. As he did, he smiled. Curious,

Sara crossed to him and stood on her tiptoes to get a better look.

"Who's that?" she asked.

"That's Miss Faye." He held the photograph so that she could get a better look.

"Oh, let me see." Careful where she stepped, Sydney made her way over to him. She wondered if he was aware of the fond note in his voice. Had he had a crush on his first teacher? She found that incredibly sweet, especially in light of the brooding face he turned to the world now.

Sara looked from the photograph to Sydney and back again. "She doesn't look like you."

"Not there, no. But in the family album there're pictures of her when she was a girl," Sydney told her. "There's a family resemblance."

"What's a re-sem-ba-lance?" Sara drawled each syllable.

Sydney smiled. "It means I have her chin and her eyes."

"And her voice." Shayne hadn't realized it until just now, listening to Sydney explain things to Sara. Sydney had the same patient tone in her voice, the same lilt as Miss Faye when she had answered her pupils' never-ending questions.

Sydney looked at him in surprise. She'd never met Aunt Faye and her father had never mentioned the similarity. "I do?"

"Yeah." He looked away, feeling as if he'd left himself too open again. "Of course, you talk a lot faster most of the time."

She grinned. "These are faster times."

They were certainly moving too fast for him, he thought.

Crossing to the crumbling wall, he tripped over a pile of dark wood and caught himself at the last minute. "What the—"

Sydney was beside him in a minute, stunned. Moving aside some of the debris, she discovered half a keyboard. She knelt to examine it more closely.

"It's a piano." She looked at Shayne. "This is her piano. What's left of it, anyway."

Mac crowded between them, elbowing Sara aside. "What happened to it?"

"Looks like a bear sat on it," Shayne guessed. The remark elicited giggles from his children, which in turn tickled him, leaving behind a warm feeling.

"What a shame," Sydney murmured. Wiping her hands on the back pockets of her jeans, she rose again.

He tried not to watch her, but it was difficult looking at anything else when she prowled around like a sleek cat, studying everything. Restless, he wanted to get going. "Seen enough?"

"Yes." Moving in a complete circle, Sydney took one last long look around. Then she turned to face Shayne. "It's perfect."

He laughed shortly. This was far from perfect by any standards. "For what, a haunted house?"

"No, to live in." If she concentrated very hard, she could envision the cabin as it had been. As her aunt had described it in her letters.

Suspicion began to ripple through him. She couldn't mean what he thought she meant. "For whom?"

"For me." Why did he look so surprised? She couldn't continue living at his house. It wasn't right. Besides, it was obvious that he really didn't want her there. As soon as she'd walked into the cabin, she'd known she belonged here. "If I'm going to remain here, I need a place to stay."

The idea of not having her underfoot wasn't quite as pleasing to him as it should have been. He tried to justify his reaction to himself. Sure, he wanted her out, but not staying in a rundown shack. Didn't the woman have any common sense at all?

"It's out of the way," he noted pointedly.

"Everything here is out of the way," she countered. There, she decided, finding a spot. She'd put her sofa right there where it would get light from the window and the fireplace. When she had a sofa, she amended, smiling to herself.

What was she grinning about? Shayne frowned. "It needs work."

She paced off the length of the room, making plans. "Nothing that can't be fixed with a little effort and some lumber." Shelves, she thought. She could put shelves in right beside the nook. Her books should be arriving soon. They were already overdue. "Fortunately, I'm pretty handy. My dad loved to work with wood, and he didn't see anything wrong in passing on his tricks to me."

The word caught Mac's attention despite his best efforts to tune everyone out. In an expression that mimicked his father's, his dark brows drew together. "Your dad did tricks?"

She placed her hand on Mac's shoulder in a gesture that was pure camaraderie. With something akin to envy, Shayne noted that the boy didn't pull away. "Sometimes, when it came to wood, he did magic."

The list of her abilities, at least as seen through her own eyes, seemed endless, Shayne mused, his mouth curving in amused cynicism. "A premed carpenter who teaches elementary school. Some would say you were becoming a very valuable asset here in Hades.''

''Some,'' she attested, looking at him over her shoulder. ''And what would you say?''

He wasn't about to comment on the effect of her presence in his life, on the town. ''I say you're biting off more than you can chew, taking this old cabin on.''

She never hesitated. ''All right, you can help me.''

She could whip things around faster than an old-fashioned turntable. ''That's not what I meant.''

''No, but it's what I meant.'' The wind's whistle was turning into a howl as it came through the large, gaping chinks in the walls. There was no doubt that the cabin was going to need a great deal of work. ''It'll go faster if there's two of us working on it.''

Sara cleared her throat. Looking down, Sydney laughed and caressed Sara's cheek. ''Three,'' she amended, then looked toward Mac. In a voice that would have done an auctioneer proud, she called out, ''Do I hear four?''

Mac looked down at his feet to hide the pleasure on his face at being included. Up until a second ago, he'd been feeling like an outsider. ''Yeah, maybe.''

She exchanged looks with Shayne. His amazement tickled her. ''I have a definite maybe. Far better than a firm no, I'd say.''

She would say, Shayne had come to realize, a lot of things. At any given moment.

''Just how in the hell did you manage all this?'' The question, directed at Sydney, was one Shayne had found himself asking—or thinking in one form or another—a lot these past few weeks.

All forms of the question revolved around Sydney.

This particular time came five days after she'd announced she wanted to move into the cabin. He wanted to know now how she had managed to rope in all the men swarming around to renovate Miss Faye's old cabin for her. Because she surely had roped them in. What had begun as a work party of four had multiplied until almost every available man, married or otherwise, had volunteered his services. Some of the men had brought along their wives, their families, and enough food to feed the whole town.

What they had here, Shayne realized, was an old-fashioned barn raising without the barn. And without electricity. The lines leading to the old cabin had long since gone down and fallen into disrepair. Several of the men had brought their own emergency generators to provide whatever power they absolutely couldn't do without.

Maybe someone should have thought of plugging the machines into Sydney, Shayne mused, because at the center of this whirlwind of activity, issuing orders in a velvety-soft voice, was Sydney who, he'd discovered, really did know her way around lumber and construction. She seemed completely tireless.

He was beginning to believe that she could do anything she claimed she could.

Sydney held a glass under the beer barrel's spigot and turned it. Beer foamed as it poured from the keg. "I just asked Ike to spread the word that I was going to renovate Aunt Faye's cabin and that I needed help," she confessed, holding the glass out to him.

He thought of passing, then decided that there'd be no harm in having just one. He'd been at this since early morning and welcomed the break.

The beer felt good, going down.

Looking around, he saw Sara playing with Bill Hanson's little girl, Gem. Even Mac had stopped hanging back and was earnestly hammering in nails under the supervision of Tate Kellogg. He looked as though he was having a good time, too.

She saw where he was looking. "Why don't you go over and help him?"

When was she going to stop interfering in his life? He hadn't asked her for advice. "Mac's doing fine on his own."

"Fine" wasn't quite the word she would have used. "A boy could always use some time with his father."

Hadn't she been paying attention these past few weeks? "Mac wants nothing to do with me."

He was wrong there, Sidney thought. "Mac wants nothing to do with the pain he's feeling inside, you just happen to be a handy target."

She debated her next words. Maybe she was overstepping a boundary that the good doctor had drawn all around himself, but she couldn't let that stop her from saying what needed to be said. After all, if things had worked out differently, she'd be family by now. She'd been raised to believe that, in the name of love, family had a right to interfere.

"Mac won't know that you love him unless you let him know."

There she went again, orchestrating his life. It was a damn good thing she was going to be moving out. "If I let him know, it won't be with a crowd of people buzzing around."

"It doesn't have to be in words," Sydney said. There were a great many ways to let someone know you cared. A touch, a nod, a thoughtful gesture. "At least, not here."

He finished his beer, then set down the mug. "You just want more work out of me."

She smiled. The man loved to grouse. It's what he hid behind, she thought. "You've already done a great deal."

How would she know that? There were men everywhere, getting in each other's way. "Watching me?"

"Noticing things. I've always paid a great deal of attention to things around me."

He had no doubts of that. Shayne wiped his hands on the back of his jeans. "You know, when you said you were handy, I didn't realize you meant that in the Tom Sawyer sense of the word. He got those boys to whitewash the fence for him by pretending he liked doing the work himself."

She knew exactly what he was driving at. "I'm familiar with Tom Sawyer." She smiled. "And Tom pretended. I'm not pretending. I really like the feeling of creating something out of rough materials. And I love the feel of wood in my hands."

"Then, darlin'," Ike announced, coming up behind them, "I'd say you came to the right place." He waved his hand in the general direction of the saw mill. "Lots of wood to be had here. Of course," he added, taking a seat on the overturned crate, "you could have picked a warmer time of year to do this. But then, just looking at you makes it suddenly seem plenty warm to me." Ike pretended to fan himself.

Sydney laughed. She'd grown to like Shayne's friend a great deal. "You make a woman feel good, Ike."

Ike raised and lowered his eyebrows, a full-blown leer on his lips as he looked her over. "You don't know the half of it, darlin'."

Shayne frowned. If she wanted to flirt with Ike, that

was her business, but he didn't have to stand around and watch. "I'll go see if Mac needs help."

She watched Shayne walk away. "I don't think he likes me very much." She wasn't accustomed to people not responding to her.

Ike helped himself to his own beer. "Funny, I was just thinking that he did."

"What gave him away, his biting off my head, or his growling at me?"

Ike laughed, giving her a chaste squeeze that left him wistful. "You're all right, darlin'."

He never addressed her by her name, Sydney noticed. "Why don't you call me Sydney?"

"Because no one with curves like yours should be called Sydney, darlin'. And as for our good doctor over there—" Ike nodded toward Shayne "—his late ex-wife did a real good number on him before she took off. And continued doing a number on him even after the divorce."

Ike knew how closed-mouth Shayne could be. While Shayne had shared a little of what had happened with him, although by no means all, he'd done a lot of reading between the lines. "He'd never been an outgoing person, so having his heart shredded by a bandsaw the one time he put himself on the line made him twice as leery of opening up." Ike studied Sydney's face, seeing more than possibly even she was aware of. "He's a good man, darlin', worth coaxing out of his shell."

Oh, no, not that tender trap. Sydney had been there twice already. "I'm really not interested in coaxing," she told him. "I've been seriously involved twice in my life and come up a loser both times. I'm not about to try for a third strike."

Ike had a feeling that this time it would be a home

run, but for now he kept that to himself. "You've got that wrong, darlin'. You weren't the loser. The men who dropped out of your life were." He winked at her, then sighed as he looked toward the staircase that was being reconstructed. "Better keep my cousin from nailing his fingers to the side of your new home. He won't be any use to me, then." He patted the side of the keg as he turned to walk away. "You think on what I said."

He left her doing exactly that.

Chapter Ten

Looking for paper, any paper, Sydney ventured into Shayne's den. He'd dropped her off at home and gone on to see a patient. Ever since renovations on the cabin had begun last week, he seemed to be trying to keep even more distance than usual between them. She knew that he wouldn't be very happy about her going through his desk drawer, but her goal was harmless enough. All she wanted was a piece of paper to make a list of things she still needed at the cabin. She had almost a houseful of furniture, thanks to donations from the people who had come to accept her as a citizen of their small town.

The cabin still needed a telephone line, and the electrical lines repaired, and the stairs still needed to be finished, but for the most part, it was almost renovated.

When she opened the first drawer, she found a jumble of papers, all with writing on them.

''You'd think a doctor would be more organized than

this,'' she murmured under her breath. But then, she'd seen his office before she'd taken over. Organization was not very high on his list of priorities.

Abandoning the middle drawer, she opened the side drawers one by one. Not a single pad was available. She'd almost given up when she discovered the box buried on the bottom of the double drawer. It was a battered box, the kind that might have once held a jacket. She opened it, though she thought she'd probably just find old medical journals or something equally as dry inside.

Instead, what was beneath the lid inside the sagging box were photographs. Dozens and dozens of well-handled photographs of all sizes. And all of the same two subjects. Mac and Sara.

She pulled out one photograph from the bottom. The date written on the back was six years old. Intrigued, Sydney flipped more photos over, pulling them out from various places within the box. He had an entire pictorial history of his children's past six years.

''Well, well, well. So you do have a sentimental bone in your body after all,'' she said smiling to herself.

''It's here, Sydney!'' Sara's boots thumped along the wooden floor as she ran into the house. The outer door banged against the wall, announcing her entrance before it sprang shut again.

Sydney's heart leaped into her throat. Quickly, she slid the lid back into place and replaced the box where she'd found it. She piled the other papers on top of it, hoping Shayne wouldn't notice the invasion of privacy. She knew he wouldn't appreciate her knowing that he had a softer side. He might not appreciate it, but she did.

Sydney looked out from the den, prepared for almost anything. Though she'd pretty much adjusted to Hades, and to her father, life was still one huge adventure for Sara.

She caught the little girl as she sailed by the den, obviously looking for her. "What's here, Sara?"

"The moving truck's here!"

The next moment Sydney found her hand firmly grasped within Sara's as the little girl dragged her to the front door.

"Van," Sydney corrected. She paused only long enough to snare her parka from the rack.

Glancing behind her, Sydney saw Mac hanging over the banister, drawn by the commotion, curious. Asia came trotting out of the kitchen, her interest piqued. Even the most minor thing became a major event in Hades, given half the chance. Boredom was as much an adversary out here as the cold, and nearly as deadly.

Sydney beckoned Mac forward. "Grab your parka and come out," she called.

There was, indeed, a large moving van parked in what amounted to Shayne's front yard. Pulling on her parka as she came out of the house, Sydney noted that the drivers were still sitting in the cab, eyeing the terrain, obviously reluctant to brave the cold.

To her it was invigorating.

Shoving her hands into her pockets, she approached the driver's side. "Where were you guys?" She'd almost given up hope of ever seeing her things again. "You were supposed to be here three weeks ago."

Resigned, braced, the driver pushed his door open, then got out. "Had some trouble with the rig. We got snowed in twice coming up the coast." It was obvious that he thought the only thing crazier than shipping possessions up here was electing to live here in the first place.

Rounding the back of the long vehicle, he hopped up on the rear platform and unlocked the double doors. The handle stuck and he wrestled with it in vain for a second before muttering a curse under his breath.

"Hey, Tom, get over here," he called to the front of the rig.

The other man, taller and broader than the driver, jumped down from the cab and made his way to the rear of the van. He gave the handle one good yank and the door opened.

The driver returned to the cab, took his clipboard from the front seat and, after glancing at the inventory that was listed, looked at Sydney. "It ain't none of my business, but you sure must want these things, considering what you paid to have them sent all the way up here."

She would have paid more. They were as much a part of her as her limbs. "I do."

"What'd they bring, Sydney?" Sara asked, hopping with excitement from one foot to the other beside her.

Sydney stepped out of the way, giving the men room. "Just some things that are very precious to me."

Boxed up within the van were her most necessary as well as her most prized possessions. Her books, her clothes, a computer, and a trunkful of photo albums that held irreplaceable photographs. Nothing that couldn't have been shipped by freight—except for one very large item that had been the deciding factor in how she would send the rest of her things.

"Let's get this over with, Tom," the driver grunted, beckoning his partner inside. "I want to get back to civilization before we run into any more bad weather."

Sara stood on her tiptoes, trying to see, but it was useless. "What've you got in there, Sydney? Tell me," she begged.

But Sydney merely grinned, knowing the value of drawing something like this out. "You'll see. Let's go inside and let these men do their job. Asia, can you get them some coffee?"

Stopping what they were doing, the men looked at Sydney as if she were an answer to a prayer.

The boxes came first. To facilitate things, Sydney had the movers pile them in the hallway, out of the way. And then came the item she'd been waiting for. The singular item whose transport here meant that she was serious about permanently sinking her roots in Alaska.

Mac's eyes grew larger than demitasse saucers. "A piano?" he cried, circling the upright's perimeter as the larger of the two men angled the dolly underneath it. Mac's mouth was all but hanging open. "You've got a real piano?"

"I've got a real piano." Sydney tried not to laugh at Mac's reaction. He'd been trying so hard to remain aloof until the movers had struggled out of the van with the piano.

Sydney greeted the sight of the honey-colored upright the way she would a long-lost friend who had finally arrived to offer her full comfort and support. It was all she could do to keep from running alongside it as the movers dollied it in. She winced as one of the corners came in contact with the wall.

"Careful with it, please," she begged.

The men didn't want to be careful as much as they wanted to be finished.

"Where do you want it?" the man called Tom huffed, struggling with his end.

Sara knew just the perfect place for it. "The living

room." As an afterthought, she pointed in the right direction.

It would look good there, Sydney thought. It was only temporary, of course, but even that would probably annoy Shayne. She looked toward the room uncertainly. "Do you think your father'll mind?"

"Lady, please, I'm getting a hernia here," the driver begged impatiently.

"My father's a doctor," Sara announced with a tinge of pride.

They were coming along just fine, Sydney thought, glancing at Sara.

"Too bad he ain't a magician, then he could levitate this thing into position," the driver cracked.

"The living room'll be just fine," Sydney assured them. It was only going to stay here until she could move into her cabin.

Once in place, Mac continued to circle the piano as if he'd never seen one up close. He raised his eyes to Sydney. "Can you play it?"

"Yes. I've been playing since I was five years old." Memories crowded through her head, memories of playing the piano, under duress at the time, on cold, snowy nights. Who knew she'd been preparing for her life out here all along?

He looked torn between admiration and suspicion. People said a lot of things that weren't true. Mac ran his hand across the wooden cover over the keys.

"Play something, Sydney."

She didn't even bother pretending that she wanted to be coaxed. In a heartbeat, Sydney was standing beside him, playing. She only paused when the driver came in with the bench.

* * *

The run had taken longer than he'd anticipated. At one point, he thought he had ice forming on his wings, but it had just been the glare of the sun hitting a water spot. For five agonizing minutes, it had given him a hell of a scare, though. Left him wondering what these people, handfuls of men, women and children scattered like grain upon the wind, would do if something happened to his plane. And him.

Someone was going to have to learn to fly this thing if Ben never came back. Kellogg's son was too unreliable. He had that look about him. The look that said as soon as he was able, he'd be gone. That left only him.

The thought linked itself up to Sydney and her never-ending pleas for flying lessons. He'd made the run without her. When she'd offered to go, as she did each time he delivered medicine and supplies to someone, he'd given her some excuse. They both knew it didn't hold up, but for once she'd surprised him and backed off. Maybe she was finally losing interest.

In any event, it had been the first run he'd made without her since she'd turned up to burrow her way into his life.

He figured he should have enjoyed the solitude a whole lot more since it had become a rare event for him. It mystified him that he hadn't. Instead of relishing the quiet, allowing it to surround him the way it had before Sydney's initial intrusion, it had somehow seemed oddly out of place for him. The solitude wasn't as comforting, it had felt…almost lonely.

He wondered if the land was finally getting to him the way it had so many others out here. A man could only take so much before he was too full of emptiness to stand it.

That his restless dissatisfaction might have had its

source in something else was a possibility he didn't want to entertain.

Getting out of the plane's cockpit, he jumped down, frowning as the sight in the distance registered. There was a moving van in front of his house. He remembered a fragment of the conversation at the airport, something about Sydney's things being packed and on their way. He hadn't given it much thought then because he'd assumed she'd be turning around to go home. But now that she wasn't—

Damn it, the house was crammed enough as it was. If she thought she could jam her furniture into his life on top of jamming herself into it, then she was in for a big surprise. She was just going to have to make other arrangements.

Exhaustion vanished as he strode toward his house as quickly as he was able. Halfway there, Shayne could've sworn he heard the sound of a piano being played. And raised voices, singing along. It linked up to a memory, but he let the chain break.

He hurried his pace. The singing grew louder. Now what?

Sydney looked up when he opened the door, their eyes meeting instantly. The sight of her smile thawed the chill that had been forming in his bones. His reaction made him twice as irritable.

"Hi," Sydney said hesitantly. She couldn't help thinking he looked loaded for bear.

She sounded awfully innocent for a woman who kept insisting on turning his world upside down, Shayne thought, gesturing at the strangers and the piano they were all gathered around. "What's this?"

"Oh, they're the movers." Sydney rose. "Dr. Shayne Kerrigan, this is Boyd Hanes and Tom Kelly."

"They brought Sydney's things," Sara chimed in needlessly.

He barely nodded in Sara's direction. His attention was riveted to the honey-colored object in the center of the living room. *His* living room. And she was leading a songfest. With movers, yet. "You didn't tell me you had a piano."

She lifted a delicate shoulder, letting it drop again. "It never worked its way into the conversation."

It was in the way of everything, couldn't she see that? No, of course not. She was in the way of everything and she couldn't seem to see that, either. Well, a man had to draw the line somewhere.

"It can't stay here."

To his surprise, she agreed. "It won't. Once Aunt Faye's cabin's finished, I'll take it there."

"How, strapped to your back?"

Sydney didn't like the edge in his voice, as if he was mocking her. When the time came, it would fall into place for her. She turned to look at him. Maybe Ike would help. "I'll find a way."

She would, too, even though he couldn't think of how offhand, Shayne knew. But somehow, he mused grudgingly, this damn stubborn woman would find a way—even if she wound up strapping Ike and Jean Luc, or any one of the dozen or so other men who came sniffing at her heels, to a sled and had them mush all the way there.

The driver looked uncomfortable at the confrontation. He picked up his jacket from the floor and shrugged into it. The other man followed suit in silence.

"Thanks for the coffee," Boyd told her. "And good luck to you." Nodding at the children, the men took their leave.

Sara and Mac ran outside to see them on their way. Shayne was surprised that Mac could be so animated.

He didn't realize that Sydney was behind him until he felt her hand on his arm. "Don't you like music?"

He turned to look at her, then felt something twist inside him. He almost came out and told her that he'd missed her today, but then thought better of it. If ever anyone could make a mile out of an inch, it was Sydney. "It has its place."

Sydney studied him for a moment, wishing she could understand him better. "But not in your life?" she guessed.

He was going to say no, that he didn't have time for such things, but then that same memory returned, stirring within him. The one that had whispered through him when he'd first heard the piano.

He merely shook his head as he walked away. "Not anymore."

Sydney crept down the stairs quietly. Mac and Sara were both asleep. She assumed Shayne was, too. It was almost eleven and his door was shut when she'd slipped out of her room just now. There was no noise, no line of light sneaking out from beneath his door. Everyone was asleep but her.

She couldn't seem to sleep tonight, though she was tired enough.

It probably had to do with having the piano arrive. She could remember playing it as a little girl, although then it had been a huge chore. She'd hated practice. The only thing that had made it bearable was the history behind the piano. It had once been her great-grandmother's, and she'd given performances on it. She and the man who was to become her husband traveled around from city to city, playing anywhere that would have them. It always made Sydney feel as if she were touching a piece of history.

She had an urge to touch it now, to reassure herself that it had really arrived safely and that she hadn't just been daydreaming.

When she came to the foot of the stairs, she was surprised to see a light coming from the living room. As far as she knew, Shayne had been the last one down here. It wasn't like him to forget to turn the lights off.

There was a reason why he hadn't turned it off, she discovered. He was still there. Shayne was sitting at her piano, his hands on the keyboard, his fingers poised. He was touching the keys, although not enough to make a sound.

She debated leaving him to his privacy. The debate was short-lived. Curiosity got the better of her. "Did you ever play?"

Startled, he jerked his head up. Preoccupied, he hadn't heard her. Damn the woman, did she have to come skulking around into his every moment?

"No, not really." Embarrassed at being discovered, Shayne started to pull the cover down over the keys.

Sydney leaned over the bench and gently pushed the cover up again. "Fakely, then?" she teased.

He knew her by now, or at least this much about her: she was going to keep after him until he told her what she wanted to know. Shayne figured he'd spare himself a lot of grief by just telling her. It was no big deal, anyway.

"Miss Faye tried to teach me."

Her mouth curved, remembering the parts of a piano they'd found in the debris at the cabin. Her father had told her that Aunt Faye loved to play. Sydney could just picture her aunt working with a very young Shayne, trying to make him feel the music in his soul. She must have thought he possessed some.

"Did she succeed?"

He shrugged. He'd never been really comfortable about talking about himself, even in a cursory manner. "I could pick out a tune or two, but that was a long time ago." He began to get up.

"Play something."

The softly voiced request lingered in the air between them, as if to draw something out of him that he felt wasn't there. She did that a lot, he realized. But this time, he was just going to walk away.

"I said it was a long time ago—"

Acting as if he hadn't said a word, Sydney stood behind him and placed her hands over his, coaxing them onto the keys.

"It's in there somewhere. Why don't you try?" Her eyes met his, her face far closer than he was happy about. "Everyone needs music in their lives."

That was what Miss Faye had said to him when she had talked him into taking lessons. She would have given them to him free, but he'd paid her back by doing chores. He had his pride. And he'd been proud, he remembered, playing for her.

The light touch of Sydney's hands over his generated a warmth through him he knew was unsafe. "I don't know about that," he muttered. Then, with a surrendering sigh, he nodded. "Remember, you asked for it."

"I'll remember," she promised, sitting beside him.

With stiff fingers, he picked out the song that inexplicably still existed in the recesses of his mind. He didn't remember the title, or even the words. It had something to do with a drunken soldier, or maybe it was a sailor. Searching for the notes, he struck the keys so slowly, it was almost impossible to string what emerged into a tune.

Or so he thought.

But as he stumbled through the song that hummed through his mind, Sydney began to mimic his movements, one complete scale higher. Grinning, she played with more assurance. A melody emerged.

"That's it." He wasn't aware that he sounded excited at the reunion.

His own fingers picked up the tempo, until they were playing a duet. Finished, pleased with himself, he sat back. Sydney's soft laughter mingled with the fading strains of the chords. It was obvious that she was delighted with his success.

"See, I told you you'd remember how to play. It's something that never leaves you, you just have to want it to come back."

A little like the ability to love, a soft voice whispered in her mind.

The grin settled into a gentle smile as she looked into his eyes. There was a deep well of emotion there. Emotion she had a feeling he refused to take so much as a sip of. She placed her hand lightly on his arm, wishing she could coax that out of him, too.

He didn't like not being able to help himself. Because if he could help himself, Shayne knew he wouldn't be doing this, wouldn't be taking her into his arms, wouldn't be tilting her head back until their lips were touching. Wouldn't even be sitting at this damn piano, playing with memories when he had more important things to be doing.

Things that didn't include kissing her and losing his

way in the current of the sensation that raced over him, sweeping him away.

The instant his mouth touched hers with an urgency that took her breath away, Sydney felt alive again. Her pulse raced as she felt the kiss deepen, widen, dragging her in. She went willingly even though she knew it was a mistake to do so. Why did she think this time would be any different?

Yet she wanted this. Had wanted it from the moment she'd walked in to find him at the piano.

Wanted it longer than that.

He finally pulled back, afraid that if he didn't, he would give in to the demands pounding through him. Demands that urged him to sweep her into his arms and take her upstairs to his room.

To lose himself, just for the night, in the sweet softness of her body....

Shaken, Sydney strove for something to say that would lighten the moment. He couldn't be allowed to think that she meant anything by this. Men with the upper hand tended to press you into the ground.

"Wow," she finally said, trying to buy some time to pull herself together. She cleared her throat as she ran her hand through her hair. "It's a good thing we didn't play 'Flight of the Bumblebee.' I'm not sure where we would have wound up."

"Nowhere," he told her sternly. "We're not going to wind up anywhere."

Sydney straightened her shoulders against the sting of his words. Well, that put her in her place, she thought, rallying. Somehow, it felt like small comfort that he wasn't leading her on.

"Right." She rose. "Well, I'd better go upstairs and get some sleep." Not that she thought she could after he'd just lowered the boiling point of her blood. She bit her lip. There seemed to be only one way to save face here, to let him see that if the kiss meant nothing to him, it meant even less to her. "I thought maybe I'd move into the cabin before it's finished. Get out of your hair..."

It was a great proposition. He had no idea why he wasn't throwing his support behind it. All he knew was that the thought of her actually leaving annoyed him as much as the thought of her moving in had. Maybe more.

"It's not a good idea to go until they can run the lines for a telephone and get the electricity going." He didn't like the idea of her being cut off like that. What if she needed someone?

She shrugged. She'd obviously worn out the little welcome that there'd been. She wasn't about to remain where she wasn't wanted. "I can make do."

There she went again, thinking of herself as some sort of superwoman, about to charm small furry creatures with a single smile. "There're all sorts of things that could go wrong, Sydney. Don't be stupid."

Her eyes narrowed. She wasn't about to be browbeaten, which was exactly what he was doing. "I'll be stupid if I want to—" With that, she turned on her heel and marched toward the stairs.

He watched her go, knowing he was looking at the back of the most stubborn woman on the face of the earth. If he had any sense, he'd just agree and be done with it. But he didn't seem to have any sense, at least, none that he was using.

Shayne knew he was going to regret what he was about to say even before the words were out of his mouth. They came out, anyway.

"If you'll stay until the cabin's really inhabitable, I'll...teach you how to fly." He mumbled the last part.

She turned around slowly, not knowing if she'd heard him correctly, or just imagined it. "What?"

He didn't want to have to say it twice. Once was bad enough. "Are you losing your hearing?"

"Maybe." She took a step toward him. Then another and another, until she was at his side, eager, hopeful. "Probably, because then I wouldn't think I'd heard you saying—"

He exhaled. Everything about this woman was difficult. "I said, if you stay, I'll teach you how to fly. I don't want to have to come out and identify your frozen corpse just because you were too stubborn to listen to sense."

She nodded in agreement, although a smile had begun to creep back to her lips. "Can't have that."

Well, if she wasn't going to bed, he was. Before he swept her back into his arms. Because this time, it wasn't going to end in a kiss.

That scared the hell out of him.

Shayne strode to the stairs, muttering a careless, "Good night," as he passed her.

A third of the way up the stairs, he heard the strains of "Happy Days Are Here Again." They accompanied him the rest of the way.

The smile that came to his lips arrived there of its own accord.

Chapter Eleven

Sydney wondered when the clinic's front door had last been oiled. It needed it badly, though she had to admit that its high-pitched squeak was better than a doorbell when it came to announcing arrivals.

She looked up as the telltale creak seeped into her very bones.

A brisk wind pushed its way into the clinic, ushering in the cold, and a small, broad-shouldered woman as if in afterthought. Sydney smiled as recognition set in. She put down her pen.

"Nice to see you, Mrs. Hatcher."

The snow-white head bobbed back a greeting as the woman trudged heavily across the clinic's outer office to Sydney's reception desk, marking her path with bits of snow that had clung to her boots and were now gracing the floor.

Every one of Ursula Hatcher's sixty-three years was

etched into her face with a blunt-tipped chisel. She'd been Hades's postmistress for the past forty-one of those years and proud of it. It was her firm conviction that news, good or bad, didn't have a prayer of spreading without her aid.

People in the area knew better than to dispute that. Most figured she was right, anyway. Though no one had ever accused her of opening the mail, whose delivery she viewed as a sacred trust, there was little doubt that Ursula either knew, or divined, what was in those letters. And she was a great deal more colorful than the local newspaper.

Sydney had met Ursula during her first visit to the general store. Ursula had inspected her the way she might have inspected a package suspected of concealing a bomb. Obviously satisfied with what she'd seen, the woman had given Sydney her seal of approval.

"Got a letter for the doc. Thought I might as well bring these along, too." Digging into the weather-beaten pouch hanging off her shoulder, Ursula pulled out a bundle of letters gathered around a medical journal. She deposited everything on Sydney's desk.

Sydney raised a brow. Everyone went to Mrs. Hatcher's corner of the general store for their mail. It was rare that she made a delivery herself.

"Going in for the personal touch?" Sydney looked her over, wondering for the reason behind the visit. "Or did you want to see him professionally?"

Ursula's laugh bordered on a cackle and ended in an amused wheeze. Fisting her hand, she thudded her chest through the layers of clothing she wore.

"I ain't never been sick yet." Her blue eyes took on a sparkle. "Wouldn't mind seeing the man personally, though."

Sydney grinned. The woman had at least thirty years on Shayne, if not more. "Isn't he just a little young for you?"

Ursula could only shake her head at the naiveté that confronted her. "He's shaving, ain't he? That makes him the right age." She held up the top letter, waving it in front of Sydney. "Thought he might want to see this one right away. Might make a difference to him."

Dropping it back on top of the pile, she turned and walked out across the puddles of dissolving snow she'd brought in with her.

Curious, Sydney looked down at the envelope. And felt her heart stop for one long moment. She recognized the handwriting instantly. Why not? She'd spent enough time waiting for letters bearing it to arrive at her mailbox back in Omaha.

Gingerly picking the envelope up, she turned it slowly around, waiting for feelings to catch up to her surprise. When they finally did, they weren't nearly as intense as she'd expected them to be. Or as hurtful. Even though it had been only a month since she'd found herself figuratively stranded at the altar, the edge on the pain had been blunted considerably.

Because he was with a patient, Sydney waited to give Shayne the letter. She wouldn't have been human if she hadn't been curious about its contents. But that was the only thing she was feeling. It pleased her.

She glanced several times at her watch as she waited for Shayne to be finished, wondering if Ben had made any mention of her in his letter. Had he experienced any sort of regret for his behavior? At this point, she'd accepted the fact that she was supposed to have arrived here and he had been merely the catalyst that brought her. Grateful to him for having taken her out of the place where she'd been, Sydney realized that she had definitely moved on with her life.

A life she felt was slowly coming together for her.

It was another fifteen minutes before the door to the examining room opened and Rob Harris came out, muttering his thanks to Shayne.

"Put it on my account, will you, pretty lady?" Harris put on his hat, covering a head that was as bald and as round as a perfect marble. "I'll catch up with you the first of the month."

The employees at the mill were paid twice a month. She'd already learned that the paycheck on the first was for bills, the one on the fifteenth for necessities and pleasure. It was then that the clientele at Salty's doubled.

Sydney made a careful entry in pen on Harris's ledger as he left the clinic. Though she'd offered Shayne the use of her computer for his office, he'd staunchly refused to be dragged into the twenty-first century. She supposed there was a certain kind of charm to that. The man was a traditionalist.

He was also stubborn as hell.

Closing the book, she took a deep breath, picked up the letter from Ben and walked into Shayne's office. She didn't quite know what sort of news she was the bearer of, but given human nature, she was braced for the worst.

Shayne was staring out the window. In the not-too-far distance he could see the forest, the one the government had strictly forbidden the loggers to touch. But he really wasn't thinking about the generations of trees there. His mind was elsewhere. In the next room, where it had no business straying.

The adage "physician, heal thyself," ran through his mind. Except that in his case, he didn't know how to go about that. How to go about stemming this all-pervading restlessness that seemed to assail him every time she walked into the room. If asked, he wouldn't even be able to pinpoint exactly where this restlessness was coming from. Or where it was going to take him. He only knew what lay at the core. Or rather, who.

He didn't have to glance over his shoulder to know she was in the room. She wasn't saying anything. That was odd. "No more patients?"

Sydney walked in slowly, like a soldier picking her way through an area she suspected was heavily mined. "You seemed to have cured everyone, at least for now." There was no way to gracefully segue into what she had to give him. "This came for you while you were in with Mr. Harris." When he turned around, she held the letter out to him. "Mrs. Hatcher brought it."

"She delivered it?"

Surprise registered fleetingly in his eyes as he took the letter from her. And then he frowned when he saw the handwriting. Ben. If he was writing, that meant he wasn't coming back in person. At least not for now.

He raised his eyes to Sydney's, wondering if she knew who the letter was from.

"Yes." She answered the unspoken question. "I know it's from him."

He stared at it for a minute, debating about just tossing it on the desk and ignoring it until later. But later had a habit of becoming now and he'd never been a coward. Just some things he didn't want to know.

Because he wasn't the only one involved here, Shayne slit the envelope open.

Sydney wanted to remain in the room, to read the letter with him. It wasn't just curiosity, she had a feeling that maybe there was something in the letter that Shayne wouldn't want to read.

As if he needed her to shield him or offer comfort, Sydney mocked. She should know better by now. She turned and walked toward the door. Before she reached the sill, she heard the sound of paper being crumpled.

"He's not coming back."

Sydney turned around to look at Shayne. He was sitting on the edge of his desk, the letter a wadded scrap of paper in his hand.

"Ben's decided to open up a practice in Seattle. Says there're a great many more opportunities there for someone like him." The words echoed in his head. Shayne laughed quietly to himself. "I suppose there probably are." He looked up to see her watching him, waiting for more. For once, she wasn't asking or probing. Maybe because she wasn't, he volunteered, "In Seattle, Ben can specialize if he wants." Though he doubted Ben had the tenacity to go that route. "Or choose just to be a regular general practitioner without the constant threat of life and death hanging over him. He can just refer people to other doctors if he doesn't want to get any deeper into a treatment."

Doctoring in Alaska didn't give Shayne that luxury. Here he had to make up his mind quickly, and sometimes he was the difference between life and death.

Shayne saw that as important. Ben saw it as a heavy burden.

Something twisted inside Sydney. She wondered if he realized just how much of himself he'd given away just then. Probably not. She crossed to him slowly, her eyes on his face. "What are you going to do?"

He shrugged, throwing the letter into the wastepaper

basket. "Same as I did when Ben was in medical school. Go on alone."

Her heart twisted again. "But you're not, you know," she said softly. He raised his eyes to hers. "You're not alone. You have Sara and Mac. The town." She paused, then added, "And for what it's worth, me."

He stepped away from the implication. From the comfort. It was a tender trap, one he'd been in before. He had no desire to be in a position to have to gnaw off his own foot to survive. "I meant as a doctor."

She didn't back off. "I meant as a person."

The moment hung between them, filled with meaning, meaning he wasn't going to allow himself to explore. Because he'd been there before and, for him, there was no going back. He'd sworn that to himself, sworn that if he ever got over the pain of losing someone he loved to indifference, he would never allow himself to be in that kind of situation again. To willingly put himself there was idiotically foolhardy and he wasn't a fool.

He wasn't anything, except disillusioned.

He glanced around her, looking into the waiting room. "Any more patients out there?"

Despite the moment, she wanted to laugh at the hopeful note in his voice. "Not a one. You know, I've got just the thing to pull you out of your doldrums." His brow rose in a silent question. "How about giving me another flying lesson?"

"I don't have 'doldrums,' so there's no need to pull me out of them." And he hardly saw giving her flying lessons as a cure for anything, except maybe common sense. "You have a warped sense of humor, you know that?"

Her eyes were lit with amusement. If she couldn't offer him a shoulder to lean on or an ear to listen, she could at least give him a little diversion. And maybe, just maybe, a smile.

"Oh, I don't know. You have to admit, teaching me to fly puts all those other thoughts right out of your head, doesn't it?"

He couldn't argue with her there. She actually had a point.

But he wasn't about to capitulate without at least a semblance of a fight. "Any patients signed up for the afternoon?"

She shook her head. "Page is completely snow white."

He was out of excuses. With Sydney around, there wasn't even anything to catch up on. Accounts, records, inventory… She'd done it all for him.

Shayne sighed in resignation. He actually didn't mind the lessons as much as he said he did, but he'd be damned if he'd let her know that. She'd probably make something of it. Something she shouldn't. Something he didn't want her to.

"C'mon, then." He took his parka from the hook. "I guess I might as well teach you."

She followed him into the outer office. "You sound as if you're going to your own execution."

He glanced at her as he opened the door. "For all I know…"

The makeshift runway stretched before her like a huge canvas. On the ground were tire marks, all crisscrossing each other, evidence of all the times she'd traversed the same area in the past hour.

The cockpit felt almost claustrophobic compared to the wilderness that waited outside. Compared to the sky above, a sky she'd yet to take her virgin run in.

Sydney tightened her hands on the wheel. "I've gotten fairly good at taxiing, wouldn't you say?"

Compliments weren't anything he gave freely, but Shayne had to admit she was doing a smooth job of it. "Fairly good," he allowed offhandedly.

The man wouldn't recognize sarcasm if it bit him on the butt. She attacked the matter head-on. "Don't you think it's time that I attempted to fly?"

The words came out slowly, as if he was weighing each one separately. "You mean, with a plane?"

What else could she have meant, flapping her arms? Sydney thought. "Yes."

"No." The answer was firm, flat, leaving, he felt, no room for argument. Then to curb the disappointment he knew had to follow, he added, "I'll let you know when it's time."

She looked at him. "No, I don't think you will. I think you're hoping that eventually, I'll get tired of asking you and give up." She pressed her lips together in that determined way of hers he'd come to recognize and expect. "Well, I have news for you, I don't intend to give up."

He pointed straight ahead, to get her eyes back on what she was doing. "You're wrong."

Did he think he knew everything? "I should know my own mind—"

Shayne had to stop her before she got rolling, knowing he didn't stand a chance of getting a word in once she got under way. "No, I meant that you're wrong that it's news to me. I've already figured out that you don't stop until you get your way."

He said it as if it annoyed him, Sydney thought. It was people with her kind of determination that settled this state he loved so much. "You know, some might find that an admirable quality."

His eyes narrowed as he looked at her profile. "And some might find it irritating."

Sydney could feel his eyes on her. She baited him. "Which 'some' are you?"

He couldn't lie any more than he could give voice to feelings. "Somewhere in the middle."

She considered that. "Well, that's better than irritating, at any rate." She heard him laugh. The sound was pleasing, even if it was at her expense. "What?" she coaxed. "Did I say something funny?"

"No, not exactly." Shayne settled back, beginning to relax. She really did have this down pat. "It's just your attitude."

He had her trained so that she expected a criticism behind every comment. "What's wrong with my attitude?"

"Nothing, it's just that I'm not accustomed to anyone sounding so positive about things." Mostly, he was privy to people grumbling. About the weather, the harsh conditions, the lack of luxuries. Ben had been one of the few who had liked it here, and even Ben was gone. "You really like it here, don't you?"

She smiled, her enthusiasm rising. "Yes. Oh, I miss the malls occasionally, and having a restaurant close by if I feel like ordering out. But mostly, I like it." She spared him a glance. "I like it very much."

He thought of Barbara and how vehemently she'd despised everything about Hades, and Alaska. Even Anchorage hadn't seemed civilized enough to her. Nothing short of New York City would do. "Why?"

Did he need reinforcement, or was he really curious about how she felt? "It's big and wide and beautiful." She spared a hand to gesture at the view in front of her. "And everything we take for granted back home is so new out here, so precious. Like telephones and electricity,'' she teased. ''It makes you take a fresh look at life and appreciate everything you have.'' She looked at him. ''And everything you might have.''

He was caught again, caught within the shimmer in her eyes. So much so that the very air had stopped moving for him.

But not the plane. At the last moment he realized that she'd ceased taxing in a circle and the plane was now heading in a direct path toward the shed.

''To the right,'' he ordered. ''To the right!''

Reflexes snapped into position. She jerked the wheel as far over to the right as she could. Sydney managed to divert the plane so that it missed the structure. But just barely.

Shayne exhaled the breath he'd been holding, grateful for the near miss. A collision would have devastated the shed, and it wouldn't have gone all that well for his plane, either.

He scowled at her, annoyed with himself. He should have his head examined for ever agreeing to this, much less suggesting it. When the plane came to a stop, Shayne took the keys away from her.

''You're not ready to fly yet.''

But Sydney seemed unfazed. ''Sure I am.''

He stared at her. Was she out of her mind? ''You almost hit the shed. How do you figure you're ready to fly?''

The answer was simple and she delivered it as if she was conducting a lesson in common sense for third graders. ''That's easy. If I'd been flying, I wouldn't have almost hit the shed. The shed's on the ground, I would have been in the air.''

At first, he looked at her, dumbfounded. Then he

started to laugh. Really laugh. Whether it was relief or tension that shed itself like skin off a snake, he had no idea. All he knew was that it felt damn good to really laugh again.

He shook his head as the laughter faded. "God, but you are something else, Sydney."

She smiled at him as if he'd just paid her a great compliment. "Nice of you to notice."

Shayne looked at her then, really looked at her. There were times he forgot how beautiful she was, and how attracted to her he was. But not for long. "I notice, all right, but I just can't do anything about it."

Sydney debated taking the compliment and letting the matter drop. She couldn't. She needed to know. "Can't, or won't?"

He was honest with her. Maybe at one time he could have fallen for her. But not now. Besides, she'd been attracted to his brother, and he and Ben were as different as summer and winter. If she loved summer, the winter would only drive her away eventually.

"Both. I've been down that route, Sydney. Almost didn't find my way back."

He could do anything he wanted to. *If* he wanted to. "If you ask me, you still haven't."

"No one's asking you." He knew that sounded too sharp. She didn't deserve that. Well, maybe she did, for delving too deep, but he was supposed to be civilized. That meant not jumping down her throat. "Sorry." He thought of how devastated she'd looked that day at the airport. The day he'd had to tell her she'd been jilted. "I suppose you have found your way back."

Maybe not all the way, she allowed, but almost. "To where I can laugh and live again, yes."

"I was in love with my wife. Really in love, for the

first and only time in my life." Shayne had no idea why he was telling her this. Only that it felt good, finally letting it out. "I grew up believing that love meant standing by someone, making it work, not giving up because things weren't going according to plan. But Barbara gave up. Gave up so easily, I felt she didn't care."

The woman had been an idiot, Sydney thought. "Did you fight for her, Shayne?"

For a second, the question didn't compute. "What?"

Hampered by the seat belt, she unbuckled it and turned to face him. "When she wanted to leave, did you fight for her? Did you try to make her stay?"

He remembered the last days, the heated words, the slammed doors. And he remembered Mac crying, frightened by the yelling and the discord. That had hurt him most of all, to hear his son crying.

Shayne banked the memories. There was no point in going over them again. "I fought with her, if that's what you mean. But it didn't do any good. She'd made up her mind to go and she went."

She reached out and covered his hand. "Taking your heart with her."

He pulled his hand away, but not immediately. Not before he felt the empathy in her gesture. "That's far too romantic a notion. When she left, I grew up. I saw the world for what it was."

No, he'd seen it for what he felt it had turned into for him. "Haven't you heard, Shayne? Adults need love, too."

She looked so sure of herself. So incredibly convinced that she was right. He could almost believe it, too. Except he knew different. "You keep talking like that and—"

"And what?" she whispered.

Damn, but he wanted her. It wasn't right—for either of them—but he did. "I don't want to have feelings for you, Sydney."

Her eyes held his. "No one's twisting your arm."

He framed her face in his hands. "Yeah, they are."

It wasn't easy kissing a would-be pilot while confined to the seat of a cockpit. But he managed.

Managed just fine, in her opinion.

Chapter Twelve

Sydney couldn't have felt dizzier than if the plane had suddenly gone into a tailspin, forming corkscrew patterns in the air. The impact of Shayne's lips was getting more and more lethal every time he kissed her. And it always left her wanting more of the same.

More of him.

With her fingers curling in his hair, she felt her body yearning for fulfillment. She wanted him. Wanted him to make love with her. Wanted him to want her the way she wanted him.

She knew she had more of a chance of the sun rising at six the next morning than getting her wish.

She struggled to ignore the wave of deprivation that washed over her as he pulled back. Very slowly, she opened her eyes and looked at him.

And knew she was in very deep trouble. It was happening. Completely without her consent, she was falling in love with him.

And he probably saw it all in her eyes. Catching her lower lip between her teeth, Sydney searched for a diversion. And then she looked over Shayne's shoulder, through the passenger window.

Relief blossomed into an amused smile. "What would people say if they saw their doctor necking in the front seat of his plane?"

He had to get better control over himself, Shayne upbraided himself. But every time he was around her, he found himself weakening just a little more.

"It's not a front seat, it's a cockpit, and no one saw. Besides, we weren't necking," he denied with feeling, "it was just a kiss."

Just a kiss. And the aurora borealis is just another mediocre scenic event. He could deny it all he wanted, but Sydney knew he had to be feeling at least part of what she was. There was too much emotion, too much protest on his part not to.

Right now, she was trying very hard not to laugh as she pointed behind him.

Feeling more than a little uneasy, Shayne turned to see Ike standing right outside the plane, a wide, wicked grin on his handsome face.

Ike tapped on the side window, beckoning for Shayne to open it.

"What?" Shayne demanded, pushing the door open. His only regret was that he hadn't managed to hit Ike's midsection with it.

"Nice to see you, too, Shayne." Ike couldn't wait to get back to the Salty with this. Making no effort to disguise his obvious pleasure at the turn of events, Ike looked at Sydney. "See you managed to finally thaw him out a little.'' He winked at her, a sense of camaraderie permeating the air. ''My money's been on you from the start, darlin'.''

Right now, Shayne hated being on the outside almost as much as he hated having attention drawn to him. ''Did you come all the way over here just to tell us about your betting propositions?''

''Hell, no.'' Ike held up the bag he'd brought with him. The item inside had to be special ordered and had just arrived at the general store. ''For your information, I came to give Sydney an early housewarming present.'' Ike thrust the bag at her. ''Didn't have time to wrap it,'' he confessed. ''But I thought you might like it right away.''

Curious, pleased, Sydney leaned over Shayne and took the bag from Ike. She looked inside. Within the bag was a box, a picture of a telephone stamped on either side.

''A telephone?'' she squealed.

Shayne glanced inside the bag. ''Looks that way,'' he muttered.

Ike's grin widened, pleased with her reaction. ''I just brought it straight from the general store. Came in an hour ago. Talk about timing.''

She realized what Ike was hinting at. Hope strummed through her. ''Does this mean the telephone lines have been strung up?''

It had been rough going, Ike reflected, but the weather had cooperated for the most part. Everything seemed to have become milder since she arrived.

''As of early this morning,'' he told her. ''Reed stopped by the Salty for some breakfast when he finished the installation. Said to tell you that you can now talk to anyone you want—weather permitting.''

One down. One to go. It was all falling into place. Sydney hugged the box to her. This was really becoming home for her. "And the electricity?" Mentally, she crossed her fingers.

Ike shook his head. "Not yet." He hated the disappointment that he saw in her eyes. "But I hear tell they're working on it. Hope to have the lines repaired before Christmas."

Christmas was less than three weeks away. In Alaskan time, that was less than a blink of an eye. "Doesn't matter. I have a phone." Her eyes moved from Ike to Shayne. "I'm invincible."

"Just don't try flying to test that theory," Shayne warned darkly, annoyed more with himself than with anyone else.

He hated this strange, possessive feeling that came over him every time someone paid attention to Sydney. She wasn't his to feel that way about; why couldn't he remember that?

"C'mere," she told Ike, who complied so quickly it elicited a harsh laugh from Shayne. Leaning over Shayne again, Sydney brushed her lips against Ike's cheek. "Thank you. It's wonderful."

Okay, he'd been a good guy long enough. Shayne cleared his throat, pointedly looking at his friend. "You two want to be alone?"

Ike took a step back, his hands raised as if he were on the wrong end of a bank robbery. "And be accused of trying to muscle in on your territory? Hell, no. I might need you someday, you quack. Just my luck you'd poison me instead of cure me."

"If I haven't done it yet, I'm not about to," Shayne growled. To point out that she wasn't his territory would have been unnecessarily embarrassing for him as well as for her. And useless on top of that, if he knew Ike. So he ignored his friend's assumption, hoping it would eventually die from lack of kindling to feed it.

Sydney had pried the box lid open and was looking at the pieces neatly tucked against one another inside a nest of packaging. "I can't wait to try this out." Impetuously, she looked up at Shayne. "Switch places with me."

He saw absolutely no reason for her to say that. "Why?"

Her mind was already three leagues ahead of her words. "Well, you won't let me fly, and flying's faster than driving."

Was he supposed to understand that? "Right on both accounts," he agreed slowly, as if he were talking to a three-year-old and choosing his words carefully. "But where are we supposed to be going?"

She held up the telephone. "I want to try it out."

He looked back toward his cabin. "You can plug it into the outlet at the house."

Holding the box against her, Sydney shook her head. "Not the same thing. I want to try it out at the cabin. My cabin." That had such a great ring to it, she thought.

Chuckling, Ike reached up and clapped Shayne on the back. "Humor the lady, Shayne."

Shayne glared down at Ike. "I've *been* humoring the lady ever since she came."

Ike's amusement only seemed to be multiplying. "Do tell."

What was the use? With both of them at him, he might as well give in or be pecked to death. Shayne got out and trudged around the nose of the plane, glaring at Ike. "Wipe the smirk off your face, Ike. It's not what you're thinking."

That only made Ike laugh again. "You have no idea what I'm thinking, old friend."

"Yeah, I do. And you're wrong."

Ike struggled to mask his face in the soul of innocence. "If you say so."

The more he protested, the worse it became. Shayne gave up.

Instead of following suit and getting out, Sydney climbed over to the passenger seat. She was buckling up again when Shayne sat in the pilot's seat. Without bothering to say anything to Ike, and without a word to her, he turned on the ignition and began taxiing the short distance he needed for the plane to become airborne.

He didn't have to say anything. His actions spoke louder than any words. She was beginning to appreciate that. She supposed he reminded her of her father in that respect. Except her father had smiled a great deal more.

Sydney hugged the telephone box to her. "Thank you."

Shayne merely grumbled something unintelligible under his breath in response. He didn't want her thanks. He just wanted to be left alone.

At the time, he really believed that.

She looked like a kid at Christmas, Shayne thought. Or maybe Easter was the more appropriate holiday.

Yes, Easter. On an egg hunt. Stirring the fire he'd lit to warm the cabin, he glanced over his shoulder and watched Sydney as she went from baseboard to unfinished baseboard, looking for the telephone outlet.

A kid looking for colored Easter eggs, that's what she reminded him of.

"Found it," she announced triumphantly.

"Congratulations."

"Sarcasm doesn't suit you, you know," she told him. Making herself comfortable on the scatter rug that had once been in Jean Luc's living room, Sydney sat cross-legged, taking the telephone pieces out of the box. With fingers flying, she quickly assembled it.

Sarcasm, he thought, was beginning to be his only line of defense against her. With the flames taking on a healthy size, he rose and crossed over to her. Amusement curved his mouth.

"You look like a woman desperate to make a call," he commented.

"I am," she confessed. Almost caressing the keys, she tapped in a number over the virgin keyboard. "This just makes me feel a little more in touch with everything."

He would have thought her manner would have taken care of that for her. He'd never met a woman more in touch with everyone around her than Sydney. Everywhere she went, people seemed to gravitate to her, to her smile, to her laugh. At the clinic, the Salty, the Championship games Hades had held at the end of last week, where everyone came out to compete in physical contests the rest of the country would only turn up their noses at. Whenever he looked into the heart of the thickest throng of people, he knew Sydney would be there.

She was a veritable people magnet.

Shayne perched on the arm of the overstuffed chair that Jaclyn Riley, the elder, had donated to help furnish Sydney's cabin.

"So who are you calling? Someone in Omaha?" A girlfriend? A past lover? The last thought teased his mind like a mosquito buzzing around his head during the wee hours of a summer's night.

Sydney merely shook her head in reply, absorbing the

sound of the telephone ringing on the other end as if she were listening to a symphony at Carnegie Hall.

The receiver on the other end was picked up, and she heard a childish voice say, "Hello?" Her smile bloomed in response.

"Hi, Sara, it's Sydney. Guess what I'm doing?" She waited for the little girl to make several guesses, then said, "I'm calling you on my new telephone. No, at the cabin, sweetheart. Yes, the one everyone was helping me fix up. It's almost ready now. Of course I'll let you use the phone when you come over here. Put Mac on, will you?" She covered the receiver. "You want to talk to him?" When he shook his head, she wasn't surprised, just disappointed.

"Hi, Mac, just wanted you and your sister to be the first to get a phone call from me on my new phone. It's up at the cabin. No, I'm not moving in yet. Soon." She glanced at Shayne. "Your dad says hi. Yes, really, he does. Okay, gotta go. We'll be home in a little while," she promised. "Bye now."

Replacing the receivery in the cradle, Sydney looked up to see Shayne watching her. She couldn't read his expression and it made her uneasy. The only time she was able to read it clearly was when he was angry about something. Usually her.

He wasn't angry now, at least she didn't think so, but she couldn't guess what was going on in his mind.

Brows drawn together, Shayne was trying to untangle the puzzle that was Sydney Elliot. He wasn't having much luck.

"With everyone you could have called back east, you called Sara and Mac, two children you talk to every day." It didn't make sense to him. "Why?"

No big mystery. "I thought they'd get a kick out of being the first people I called. And I was right."

That still didn't explain it for him. The telephone was for communication, for spanning long distances, not for pleasing two kids. "You know, I don't understand you, Sydney."

He was delving too deep for an answer that was so close to the surface it almost floated. "I speak a fairly clear form of English." She smiled up at him. "What's not to understand?"

Something that had been nagging him ever since the beginning. "What I don't understand is what you're doing here."

She could have easily risen to her feet on her own. Instead, she put out her hand, waiting for him to help her up. "You know what I'm doing here. I came to marry your brother."

Taking her hand, he pulled her to her feet. "You could have turned around and gone home."

She shrugged a bit too carelessly in his estimation. "I wanted something new, remember?"

For once he wouldn't let a subject drop. This one time, he was determined to satisfy his curiosity. "Most women buy a pair of shoes when they feel like that, not a whole new way of life."

She shoved her hands into her back pockets, looking off. There were storm clouds gathering beyond the big bay window. She wished he'd stop pushing for an answer. "Maybe I needed that whole new way of life."

"Why?" he persisted. "I'm trying to understand why a woman who can obviously make friends wherever she goes would want to go into hiding."

Her chin jerked up. "It's not hiding, it's..." Oh, what did it matter? "My father died almost three years ago, and it devastated me. For the first time in my life, I felt as if I was adrift. And alone," she admitted. "Very alone." She took a breath. Even now, it was painful to go over it. To touch upon her mistakes. "Then I fell in love with the wrong man—"

"My brother." He meant it rhetorically. He didn't expect her to shake her head.

"No, this was someone before your brother." She could see that she'd surprised him. Well, he'd asked. "Someone your brother helped me to forget with his letters." Letters that were so important to her, that had helped her out of the very difficult place she'd found herself in.

"What happened? With the other man, I mean."

She shrugged. "I wanted children, he wanted freedom. I thought we hit some sort of a compromise. He left me at the altar." She sighed. That was all behind her now. "I thought that maybe things happened for a reason and I was meant to go through what I had in order for Ben to come into my life." She rocked back on her heels, looking back and feeling foolish. "But I thought wrong."

Twice, she'd been left at the altar, figuratively and literally. And yet she was still forging ahead. He wasn't sure whether to admire her, or call her a hopeless fool.

Raising her chin, she almost looked defiant to Shayne. "My track record as far as making emotional choices is zero for two. So I've decided to stop looking for someone to share my life with and just live it instead." It seemed like a safe, sane way to go. "So far, I think I'm doing pretty well."

The firelight was playing on her hair, making it look as bright as the golden nuggets that had brought prospectors running in droves at the turn of the century. He

would have been less than human if he could have resisted touching it. And he suddenly felt very human. He
shifted a strand through his fingers, his eyes on hers.

"You know, sometimes they say when you stop looking so hard for something, you find it."

She felt as if her heart had gotten lodged in her throat.
"What are you saying?"

Very slowly, he moved his head from side to side.
"Damned if I know. Just like I don't know why I want
to keep kissing you."

Her smile spread from her lips to her eyes. To him.
"Don't they teach elementary biology to med students
anymore?"

God, but he wanted her. Wanted her so badly, it almost hurt. "I slept through that class."

With less than a breath between them, she wound her
arms around his neck.

"Oh, then let me give you a refresher course. It says
that men and women are inherently attracted to each
other." Her body leaned into his. "I think it has something to do with a theme and variation on that axiom
about opposites attracting." *Kiss me, Shayne. Don't
make me throw myself at you.*

He laughed softly, trying very hard not to give in to
the heat he felt flaring through his body. "You might be
on to something there. We're as opposite as two people
can get."

"Absolutely." She took a breath, and then there was
nothing between them, not even air. "You want to talk
about the theory of relativity now, or are you going to
kiss me?"

The resistance he thought he had against this sort of
thing was melting faster than snow in July. "Physics was
never my strong suit."

"Thank God."

She knew. Standing in this cabin where her great-aunt had once taught, Sydney knew. Knew as soon as he touched his lips to hers that this time it was going to be different. This time, short of an avalanche, there'd be no interruptions, no excuses to intrude and stop either one of them from the natural path they were on. Nothing could stop them, except perhaps common sense, and that was in pitifully poor supply on her end.

She didn't want to think about consequences, or the fact that kissing him, allowing her body to heat to the temperature of a roaring fire, was one of the most fool-hardy things she'd ever done. Because right now, it wasn't foolhardy. Right now, it was wondrous and thrill-ing.

Shayne didn't know what it was about Sydney that made him lose his ability to think, to reason, to act ra-tionally. All he knew was that if he couldn't have her, couldn't feel her soft body pliant and giving beneath his, he was going to go out of his mind.

He was going there anyway, but the route, he discov-ered, was a great deal sweeter than he'd ever anticipated.

Molding her to him, his mouth deepening the kiss with each pass, Shayne felt her tremble against him. In fear? The possibility throbbed in his brain.

Though it was the most difficult thing he'd ever done, he pulled his head away from hers and looked at her. Trying to find a clue. He couldn't just come out and ask her.

The ache within her was growing to proportions that were almost unmanageable. She drew a breath, trying to steady her rapidly beating pulse. It did no good.

Was something wrong? Had he suddenly changed his mind at the last minute? She searched his face. He wanted her. She could see it. So why had he stopped? "Is justifiable homicide on the books in this state?"

It was the oddest question he could conceive at a time like this. "I think so, why?"

"Because…" she pressed her lips to his neck. "If you stop kissing me now—" spidery kisses circled his collarbone, tightening his gut, teasing his loins "—I'm going to be forced to kill you."

She was clouding his mind, heating his blood, breaking the last bands of his restraint. He struggled to hold off. "Sydney, maybe we shouldn't."

It was like a cold knife twisting in her gut. She raised her head and looked at him. Had she been wrong, after all? "Do you want to stop?"

Shayne couldn't have lied even if salvation lay in the balance. "No. Heaven help me, but no, I don't."

She could have cried. "Then don't. Don't stop," she whispered, the sound skimming along his skin. Signaling his doom.

And his victory.

Lowering his mouth to hers, Shayne kissed her as if his very soul was behind it. Because it was. He'd only just now discovered that he still had a soul and that it was alive and, if not well, possessed by needs.

What followed he would remember all the days of his life, no matter how many there would be. The urgency he experienced was almost overwhelming. Certainly overpowering. He didn't even try to resist.

They undressed one another in a synchronized symphony. Clothing instead of notes rained through the air, floating to the floor below.

Each newly exposed region he discovered on her body made him feel like an explorer, claiming a new territory for crown and country.

And for himself.

Shayne didn't delude himself into thinking he was her first and knew he wouldn't be her last. But for now, he was here with her and she was his and that was more than enough.

It was just right.

Her skin felt creamy beneath his hands as he skimmed first his fingers, then his palms over her smooth, naked flesh. She arched and moved in response to his every touch, silently urging him on. She was like a woman possessed. Shayne fanned the flames, kissing her over and over again, undoing her. Undoing himself.

He'd been married. Known, he thought, all the pleasures of the flesh that were to be had.

He knew nothing.

He learned everything, driven by the need to take his pleasure with her. To give her pleasure. He had no idea which gave him more satisfaction.

Laying her back on the rug, he followed each path he'd forged with his hands with his lips, thrilling at the sound of her moan, feeling suddenly empowered, reborn in the glisten of her skin as it caught the light from the fireplace.

The thrill he felt at touching her was more than matched by what he felt when she moved suddenly and switched positions. Now it was Sydney who was over him, Sydney who toyed, teased and suckled.

As her hands played over him, first lightly then more and more possessively, skimming his chest, his flat stomach, his thighs, he could feel everything within him tightening like the string stretched over the bridge of a guitar. Tightening and pulsing. Waiting for the grand moment when the final notes of the melody could be struck.

Wanting to hold them off forever.

Wanting to hear, to feel them now. Feel them vibrating through his body.

Knowing that if she continued what she was doing, her hands feathering along the muscles of his inner thighs, her fingertips possessing him, he wouldn't be able to hold back much longer, Shayne deftly moved so that she was beneath him again.

He made love to her with every fiber of his being, consumed with the desire to eliminate every other man from her mind. He caressed, possessed, nipped, kissed, and marked her indelibly as his.

She stored every sensation greedily within her, to be replayed and savored time and again, during future long nights when dawn seemed years away. He made her feel beautiful, wanted and happy. So exquisitely happy she thought she was going to burst.

To repay him, to revel in the sensations they shared, she found herself loving his body in ways she'd never dreamed. Because he made her want to do things, pleasuring things, just by the way he made love with her.

A twig snapped in the fire's greedy jaws as the first explosion Shayne created within her racked her body, exhausting her. Making her crave more.

And more again.

Shayne anticipated and provided, leaving her gasping. Leaving her dazed. Again and again he raised her to the highest plateau, taking her up and over. And then safely down, only to begin again.

She couldn't take any more. Not alone.

Sydney reached for him, blindly grasping his forearms and weakly dragging him to her. Anticipation danced through her as his body moved along the length of hers, into position.

With what seemed like her last ounce of strength, she smiled at him. "I know you can revive me if I pass out, but I want to be awake for this." She arched her hips, the invitation unmistakable.

He accepted it, sheathing himself in her and finding so much more than he had ever dreamed possible. It wasn't just the exquisite meeting of flesh to flesh, of needs to needs. Even the passion didn't explain it. It was the feeling that something far more momentous was happening that made this so wondrous.

Though he knew it was absurd to harbor the sensation, he couldn't shake the feeling that he was coming home, finally home. And for now, he didn't want to shake it. He wanted to savor it. Savor it the way he savored the sweetness of her mouth, the sensuality of her scent as it filled every part of him.

As it possessed him.

Together, the rhythm of their bodies growing frenzied, they found what they were each looking for.

For now.

Chapter Thirteen

A chill was beginning to creep into the room, slowly, like a cat checking out the premises for future habitation. Or maybe it'd already settled in and she was only just now noticing.

Sydney sighed, looking at the flames. "The fire's dying out."

He couldn't remember ever having been this exhausted. But feeling Sydney stir beside him, her breath lightly gliding along his skin as she spoke, was beginning to bring him around again.

"Give me a minute and I'll see what I can do about it."

Sydney raised herself up on her elbow, turning toward him. Her hair rained down on his chest, lightly skimming it with every movement like the soft flutter of an angel's wings.

Her mouth curved wickedly. "Promises, promises. I'd

say that what just happened now will warm me for a very long time to come.''

He felt like kissing her again. Like making love with her over and over the whole night long. He was too tired to realize that this was a first for him.

Shayne eyed the fireplace behind her. ''Which fire are we talking about?''

Her smile grew, taking him with it. ''Whichever one you want. Both, if you like.''

Duty and desire waged a quick battle within him. Duty won. But there was no winner, not in the real sense. ''What I'd like…''

She looked at him hopefully, not completely sure what it was she was hoping for. Only knowing that she needed to hear something positive from him, however small. ''Yes?''

For just a second longer, he tried to hold on to the sensation he'd felt making love with her. But it was already fading. ''What I'd like and what I have to do are two very different things.''

Sydney sat up, resigned. ''Not where I thought this conversation was going,'' she confessed with a sigh. She dragged a hand through her hair. ''But you're right, we have to get back to the children.'' She reached for her underwear and quickly wiggled into it, then began pulling on her jeans. ''I don't know if Asia can handle them both.''

He shouldn't be watching her get dressed, he should be getting dressed himself. His hands remained idle, his body heating. ''Not since you breathed life into them, at any rate.''

She cocked her head, scrutinizing him. ''Is that a compliment or a criticism?'' There was no clue in his voice, but she was getting used to that. With Shayne, you needed all your senses alert.

Getting up, he pulled on his jeans. He glanced over his shoulder in her direction. "Whichever one you like."

This time she heard the amusement in his voice. "Sorry, that quote's already been taken. Have to come up with one of your own, I'm afraid."

"And I'm afraid…" He turned just in time to see her slipping her sweater on over her head, her torso stretched. She'd neglected to put on her bra. His mouth turned to cotton.

Sydney yanked the sweater down so she could see again. "Yes?"

He let out the breath he was holding. His chest hurt, and the cause, he knew, was not rooted in anything remotely medical. "And I'm afraid that I can't seem to put two thoughts together anymore."

She saw how he looked at her and she smiled, pleased. Flattered. And wishing there was enough time to make love all over again. She stepped closer to him. "You're too young to be senile."

Urges, freshly satisfied, freshly tantalized, began to rise again for Shayne. Damn, but he could feel the heat of her body, even with space between them. "Is that your professional medical opinion?"

She laughed, splaying her hands over his chest. Leaning into him.

"Call it a gut feeling." Shifting, she moved against his side and he winced in reaction. The response occurred in less than a split second. Concern nudged her. "What's the matter?"

The pain came suddenly, sharply. Taken by surprise, Shayne concentrated on regulating his breathing. The pain began to fade. "Nothing."

It didn't look like "nothing" to her. He looked as if someone had just jabbed him with a cattle prod. "You winced."

He shrugged it off, wishing she wouldn't insist on making something out of everything. The pain was already a memory.

"A stitch," he insisted. "Nothing more."

And he wouldn't tell her even if it was, Sydney realized. No sense in her butting her head against this iron wall.

"You're the doctor, you should know." She refused to let anything mar what they'd just shared. The euphoria was still wrapped around her like a coat of airtight iron armor. Sydney raised her eyes to his. "I had a very nice time installing the telephone."

Even wanting, for simplicity's sake, to put what they'd just done behind him, Shayne couldn't help but laugh. "Is that what you call it now?"

She nodded, her eyes still on his. "From now on."

From now on. That had such a permanent ring to it.

But he knew there was no such thing as permanent. Barbara had shown him that, and so had Ben. And each had had a great deal more invested in his life than Sydney did. In comparison, he and Sydney were almost strangers.

Strangers who had made exquisite love together.

But still strangers.

Sydney frowned, looking up at him. Her euphoria began to slip away. "I know that face. It's your pessimistic face."

He frowned in response, then realized it was only reinforcing what she said. "I don't have a pessimistic face." Frustrated, he turned and began looking for his shirt. It had to be here somewhere.

Sydney followed him. "Yes, you do. I would have said it was your regular face, except that I've seen you look differently, so I know you don't have to look like that if you don't want to."

It took him a minute to untangle the words. He didn't know which was worse; that she rattled on, or that he could actually follow her with a little effort. "I'm not a pessimist, I'm a realist."

"You're a pessimist," she insisted, her tone mild. "I'm an optimist. To me, the glass is half full and there's a waitress coming toward me with a pitcher, ready to fill it. Your glass is half empty and not only don't you see the waitress but you also think she's quit and taken the pitcher with her."

She was right, he thought. But that still just made him a realist. He shrugged into his shirt. "Are you through?"

Sydney began to close his buttons for him. "For now."

He moved her hands aside and finished the job. If he let her do it, he wouldn't be able to force himself to leave.

"One clings to small favors." He picked his parka up off the floor. "Let's go before it gets too dark."

Sydney slipped on her parka. "I've got a feeling it already has."

Shayne wasn't about to ask her what she was talking about. He didn't think he wanted to know.

With a sigh, Shayne closed the medical journal he'd been trying to read and massaged the bridge of his nose. He was having trouble concentrating.

It was all her fault.

In more ways than just one. The noise echoing outside his window—a noise Sydney had incited and for which she was directly responsible—made reading hard enough on its own. He could ignore that.

What he couldn't ignore was the way she lingered in his thoughts, how she'd burrowed into his life and set up residence like some Arctic hibernator. Burrowing in and giving him no peace.

She intruded on every facet of his life, physically and otherwise. Even here, in his den. The things the moving men had brought were being stored in this room until she made her final move into the cabin.

He could swear her perfume was on every one of the damn items. Even on the piano in the living room. Never mind that she'd said she didn't use any, it was here, haunting him. Reminding him of the one afternoon where discretion and his good judgment had left him. An afternoon more than a week in the past now.

Reminding him that, common sense not withstanding, he wanted her again.

He wished she'd moved out already. But that was his fault. She would have been living in Miss Faye's cabin by now if he hadn't bribed her into waiting with those flying lessons. But something inside him just couldn't ignore her.

What was the matter with him? She got underfoot, wedged herself into places she had no business being. Interfered with everything. He should have been glad for the opportunity to get rid of her.

And yet, he wasn't.

He didn't like the idea of her living out there all alone. Didn't like the idea of her leaving. And liked, even less, that it bothered him the way it did.

Damn it, he knew where such attachments led. Into gaping black holes. Why was he even thinking this way?

Because he couldn't help himself.

Yet.

But he would, by God, Shayne vowed silently. He would.

Shayne jumped at the sound of the sudden, unexpected "thud" that smacked against his window, rattling it. The next moment he saw Sydney peering in, her face reddened by the cold and the wind. Brightened with laughter he could only partially hear. She waved at him and mouthed an exaggerated, "Sorry." The remnants of the snowball she'd thrown clung to the pane. And then she disappeared.

Curious, Shayne opened the window to see where she'd gotten off to and inadvertently offered himself up as the perfect target. Another white missile flew through the air. This time, without the glass to stop it, it went crashing into his face.

Her laughter echoed loud and clear this time. Winding all through him. There was a chorus of childish laughter in its wake. Sara and Mac.

"C'mon out," Sydney crowed, beckoning to him. "The snow's fine!"

"The hell it is." He wiped the last of snowball from his face.

Shayne had no idea what possessed him. The last time he'd been in a snowball fight, he'd been ten, maybe eleven. After that, life had gotten too serious. But he hurried out now, grabbing his parka, determined to wash her face in snow and pay her back.

Sara was the first to see him. "Daddy, did you decide to play with us, after all?" She clapped together snow-covered mittens in excitement.

Shayne stopped long enough to pick up a handful of snow and mold it between his gloves. "Just for a few minutes. Just long enough to pay Sydney back."

Standing a good distance away, Sydney stuck out her chin, daring him to hit it. "You probably throw like a girl."

The next second, shrieking with laughter, she ducked out of range. He missed.

He didn't miss the second time. Or the third. Victorious, having done what he'd set out to do, he thought the battle over.

He thought wrong.

Sydney was more than ready for him with a cache of snowballs, waiting to be hurled, at her disposal. The wait was over the second Shayne's third snowball hit its target. Winding up, she began depleting her arsenal at an incredible speed.

Mac, his eyes bright with enthusiasm, rushed over to join Sydney. In less than a few minutes, the air was thick with snowballs.

Sizing up the situation, Sara threw her lot in with what she deemed in her young heart to be the underdog. Ducking her head, she scurried over to him. "I'll help you, Daddy."

"I appreciate it," Shayne told her, although he knew that Mac would be much better at snow warfare than his sister. Sara threw a malformed snowball that landed a foot away from her.

Just his luck, Shayne thought, but he smiled and said, "Good try."

Mac's snowball made the distance, squarely baptizing his sister in the face. She gasped and Shayne expected the confrontation to instantly break down into yelling and tears. Instead, he heard Sara laugh and rush to make another snowball.

His surprise cost him. Sydney hurled two snowballs

in quick succession, striking him with a one-two punch. Shayne held his hands up in front of his face.

"Uncle!"

"Aunt!" she yelled, hurling another one at him.

Shayne saw the arsenal that was still left. She was equipped to keep this up for half the afternoon. He saw no other avenue open to him. He could either stand and be pelted, or charge her.

He chose the latter and ran straight into Sydney, grabbing her by the waist and sending her crashing down into the snow. Perforce, he went with her. It was a small sacrifice to pay. And an enjoyable one, layers of clothing notwithstanding.

The next thing he knew, the children had piled themselves on top of both of them. The laughter and squeals fed into one another until it all formed one harmonious sound.

Music to his ears, he realized, pleasure spilling through him.

He struggled to his feet, succeeding on his second try, which necessitated untangling his body from his children. Shayne offered Sydney his hand. "I had no idea you were this bloodthirsty."

Sydney accepted his hand and found herself unceremoniously yanked upright. "A lot about me you don't know." Cheeks glowing, she paused to brush the snow out of her hair. She slanted a look at his face to see what he made of her comment. "The nights are long, maybe you'll learn."

"Maybe," he agreed. The remark was accompanied by a careless shrug.

His tone sounded ambiguous, but she supposed his answer was better than a silent reproof. In any case, Sydney let it be.

Dusting the snow off her legs and rear, Sydney looked around for Sara and Mac. Collectively, there was more snow on them than on the chalet roof. "Okay, who's for hot chocolate?"

Sara raised her hand excitedly. "I am."

It wasn't cool to be too excited. But Mac's eyes gave him away. "Me."

Shayne stared at her. "We have hot chocolate?" Since when? he wondered.

She looked at him, surprised that he thought she'd be careless enough to make promises, however small, without backup.

"Of course we have hot chocolate. What kind of a sadist would offer children hot chocolate if there wasn't any?" she teased. "Mr. Kellogg got in a whole case for me."

Of course he did, Shayne thought, surprised the general store owner hadn't ordered a private cow for her, as well. Everyone tried to be so damn accommodating to Sydney. "How much hot chocolate do you intend to drink?"

The smile on her face was enigmatic. "Nights get cold here."

He had no idea if she was mocking him or not.

The sound caught Sydney's attention. At first she dismissed it, thinking that it was just the wind winding its way through the trees. She'd learned to tell the difference now between the mournful sound of the wind and other things that were only close in timbre.

She listened again, harder. It was the sound of crying. Muffled crying.

One of the children was crying. Curious, moved, she crept softly into the hallway and listened, holding her breath so she could hear more clearly. There was nothing.

Her imagination was playing tricks on her. Turning away, she headed toward the stairs when the sound came again, escaping like a fugitive bound for freedom. It was coming from Mac's room.

Sydney tried Mac's door and found it wasn't locked. She debated, only for a second, giving him his privacy. But he was a little boy who needed comfort more than he needed a space to call his own. Pushing the door open slowly, she found Mac lying on his bed, his face buried in his pillow. The sobs escaped anyway.

She approached with caution, knowing that the Kerrigan men were a pride-laden lot, even the smallest one. "Mac, are you all right?"

Mac hunched his shoulders together, as if trying to sink further into his pillow. He refused to turn his head. "Go away."

She didn't budge. Instead, she placed her hand on his shoulder and felt it stiffen. He and his father had a great deal in common. "Mac, what's wrong?"

"I said go away." He sniffed, hard. Then the accusation came. "That's what you're going to do anyway, right? So go away now." He raised his head to look at her, tear tracks down both cheeks like war paint. "I mean it, go away."

Instead of leaving, Sydney sat on the edge of his bed. "I'm not going to go away. Not until I find out what's bothering you. And not even then."

He said nothing. And then, finally, struggling with his feelings, he looked at her again. "Then you're not moving out?"

So that was it. He thought she was abandoning him. She knew how hard it had been for him to reach out to her in the first place. She ran her hand along his hair, smoothing it. "Yes, I'm still moving out. But I'm not going away. I'll still be here in Hades. And I'll come see you and Sara every day if you want."

"How?" He stuck out his lower lip belligerently. "It's too far."

"It's not too far with a car."

"But you don't have a car."

"I will soon." She saw the surprise on his face. "I ordered one, and they're sending it all the way from Detroit."

It hadn't been an easy process. It wasn't like a large city, where she could have gone to a local dealer and pick out a car. She'd made her choice from a pamphlet, basing her decision on Shayne's judgment by ordering the same kind of vehicle he used. She'd bought the car on her own, without his knowledge. She'd figured it was one less thing to bother him about.

"Is that going to take time?"

She saw the hopeful look in Mac's eyes and it tugged on her heart. Why couldn't his father look at her that way? "Everything takes time here."

The answer satisfied him. Mac manfully brushed away the wet streaks his tears had left on his face. He looked at her sheepishly. "Pretty dumb, huh? Crying like a baby."

She couldn't help herself any longer. She hugged him to her. It touched her that he let her. "Babies aren't the only ones who cry, Mac. I cried when my dad died. A great deal. And men cry."

He shook his dark head. He knew better. "Men don't cry."

She crooked her finger beneath his chin and raised it

so that their eyes met. "Oh, yes, they do. They have feelings just like you do. Things hurt them."

Maybe some men, Mac allowed. But he knew of one who remained above all that. Above things like hurting and tears. And feeling scared.

"Not my dad. He doesn't have any feelings. Except maybe the hating kind." Mac pressed his lips together, wondering if he'd said too much.

Oh, God, was that what Mac thought? She took his face in her hands and said very carefully, "He doesn't hate you, Mac. He loves you and he loves Sara. Very, very much. He just doesn't know how to say it, that's all."

The big, dumb ape, she thought in silent frustration.

Sydney was just trying to be nice. He had proof that he was right and she was wrong. "He doesn't love me. He never came once to see me, not until after...after Mom died."

She gathered the boy to her, wishing there was some way she could shield him.

"He didn't come to see you because he couldn't. Your mother didn't want him to." It was a fine line she was walking and she knew it. Not wanting to upset any of Mac's memories of his mother, Sydney tried to remember what Ike had told her. "She did it because she thought it was best for you and your sister not to have your dad come in and out of your lives. Your dad thought you'd be okay if he did, and they argued about it. He decided not to try to see you because he didn't want the shouting to upset you." She caressed his hair. "They both loved you very much."

There were fresh tears forming. "I don't think so."

There had to be some way to convince him. And then she remembered. "If your dad didn't love you, he wouldn't have kept all those pictures of you in his desk.''

"He's got pictures of me?"

"Tons of them. Pictures of you and Sara. I'd say there were probably six years' worth." She saw his eyes light up. Bingo. "I bet your dad spent a lot of nights just sitting in his chair, looking at those photographs over and over again. Missing you. Thinking he'd never get to see you again.''

A warm feeling came over Mac, like when Sydney tucked him into bed and made the blanket all snug around him when it was cold. "How'd he get the pictures?"

He wasn't suspicious, she thought. He just wanted to know. "When someone loves someone else, they find ways.''

Mac wanted to believe her, he really did. There was just one final question. "How do you know my dad has pictures?"

"I saw them. I was looking for some paper one day and found them in a box in his bottom drawer," she confessed. She'd never said anything to Shayne. She knew he wouldn't have appreciated her going through his things, but even if he found out, the look she saw on Mac's face now, made the risk worth it for her. "The deep one.''

He wriggled off the bed. "Show me."

The boy clearly had Missouri blood in him. This made discovery almost a sure thing. Sydney debated, but the hope in Mac's eyes cut the debate short.

"My pleasure." She took his hand and they headed for the door.

Chapter Fourteen

"What are you doing?"

Startled, Sydney looked up to see Shayne standing in the doorway. She hadn't heard him come into the house. Anticipating a scene, she moved from the desk where she and Mac had been looking at the photographs and placed her body between Shayne and his son.

"Mac didn't believe that you had photographs of Sara and him in your desk." She glanced at the pile in front of Mac. "I could put them into an album for you if you'd like."

Shayne had come home exhausted. The single patient he'd gone to see in the Inuit village had mushroomed to twelve. Though he hated admitting it, he'd sorely regretted not taking Sydney up on her offer to accompany him. Just having her around seemed to put people at ease. But he'd wanted to become less dependent on her, not more.

The light coming from his den had drawn him there instead of to the kitchen for food to placate his growling stomach. He hadn't expected to see her going through his things with his son.

"What I'd like, Sydney, is for my things to remain where I put them." Shayne frowned, looking at the contents scattered all over the top of his desk. "How did you know they were there?"

Sydney heard the accusation, sharp and cold in his voice. It wasn't a voice belonging to a man she'd made love with such a short while ago.

Served her right for thinking that anything had changed between them. Or that they had a future together.

Just her luck, she thought, to be doomed to give her heart to men who didn't want it. She stepped closer to him, lowering her voice. She didn't think she could be held responsible for what she'd do if he somehow ruined this for Mac. "That doesn't matter right now. What does, is that Mac knows you care about him."

What gave her the right to presume to know how to run his life? Why did she think she could just interfere in it anytime she felt like it? "He doesn't need to find photographs for that."

The look in her eyes cut him dead. "Everyone needs physical evidence of some sort."

Unaware of the storm brewing around him, Mac held up a photograph. "What does this say?" His question temporarily broke the tension.

Not trusting himself to say anything more to Sydney, Shayne crossed to his son and took the photograph from him. He looked at the back, then paused, reading the notation. It was in his own hand. Barbara had never bothered writing anything on the back. But as soon as he received them, he'd meticulously written dates and events on the back of every photograph she'd doled out to him so stringently.

"'Mac, first day of school.'" And then he read the date. Mac was smiling into the camera, his wide grin shy, one tooth in the front. He clutched a lunch box in one hand, a notebook in the other. Shayne remembered the pride he'd felt looking at that photograph. Pride mixed so strongly with resentment because he couldn't be there in person to witness it. Resentment because Barbara had barred him from his own children.

Mac took the photograph back and examined the writing. He shook his head. His dad must've flunked penmanship. "You've got funny handwriting."

The remark, so guilelessly tendered, made Shayne laugh. "I'm a doctor. I'm supposed to have funny handwriting."

Mac looked at the box. There were a great many photographs still in there, as well as the ones spread out all over the desk. The eyes he raised to his father forbade Shayne to lie.

"Why did you keep these?"

Shayne could feel Sydney looking at him, waiting for him to answer Mac. He didn't like explaining himself, but he knew his son's needs outweighed his own feelings in this case.

"Because I couldn't be there to see it happening first-hand." It cost him to bare his soul like this. "I asked your mother to send them to me. I wanted to see what you and Sara looked like while you were growing up."

Mac rolled every word over in his head, examining it carefully from all angles. He needed to be sure. "So you really did care?"

Shayne exchanged looks with Sydney. She was right,

damn her. Mac needed to hear this, needed to be told and shown that he mattered. It wasn't enough to assume that he understood.

Emotion filled him as he gathered his son to him, trying to make up for lost time. Knowing it wasn't possible. But at least he could try. "I did and I do."

Shayne heard the door close behind him. When he looked, he saw that Sydney had slipped out of the room. He'd underestimated her. She knew that some things required privacy.

Like a man getting reacquainted with his son.

Just when he thought he had the woman pegged.

Arms tightening around Mac, Shayne did his best to reassure the boy. Privacy or not, the words didn't come out any more easily. But he knew that they had to be said.

"Just because I wasn't there, Mac, didn't mean I didn't care. Didn't mean I wasn't thinking about you and your sister every minute of every day."

Mac looked up and studied him solemnly. Shayne could see that the boy really wanted to believe him. "Every minute?"

Shayne nodded, running his hand through the boy's hair. He couldn't help thinking how much Mac looked like Ben when Ben had been his age. "Every minute."

An almost imperceptible twinkle entered Mac's eyes. "Even when you were sleeping?"

Definitely Ben material. There'd been a great deal about his brother that had been lovable, Shayne remembered. "They're called dreams, then, wiseguy." Shayne laughed, tousling the boy's hair.

Mac grinned. "I dreamed about you, too. Lots of times."

Shayne doubted very much if Mac could have said

anything that would have meant more to him than what he'd just said.

Shayne spent a long time in the den with Mac, poring over photographs, talking. Discovering. The exhaustion he'd felt earlier when he'd arrived home peeled away from him like an outer covering that was no longer pertinent or in vogue.

He knew he had Sydney to thank for this. But how did he thank someone for invading his space, his privacy?

Nothing about the woman was simple.

Leaving Mac to return the photographs to the box, Shayne walked out of the den, looking for Sydney. He had to admit that it surprised him that she had left the two of them alone for so long. He'd half expected her to come in, ready to mediate or just place herself in the center of what was going on.

The woman was a complete enigma to him. He didn't know whether to shake her or hug her. Or both. No matter what he was doing, Sydney somehow managed to inspire such diametrically opposed emotions within him, it set his head spinning.

He wondered if she did that on purpose.

The strains of chords being slowly picked out on the piano came to him almost as soon as he opened the door. Shayne followed the sound to the living room.

Which was where he found her.

Sydney was sitting at the piano, sharing the bench with Sara. With a look of total concentration, Sara was trying to mimic Sydney's fingering on the keyboard.

Sydney looked up the moment he entered the room though he made no sound. It was as if she were somehow aware of his every movement. He wouldn't have been surprised if she were.

Sydney tried to read his expression. He didn't look annoyed. At least that was a good sign. "So, how did it go?"

"Well," he said slowly.

Maybe it was small of him, but he couldn't let her invasion pass lightly. If he did, he had a feeling that the incident would only repeat itself and mushroom to unmanageable proportions. And he didn't want her entrenched in his life any more than she already was.

As it was, she'd already upheaved the life he thought he'd made for himself.

Shayne crossed to the piano, to Sydney's side of the bench. He lowered his voice to keep from distracting Sara. "That still doesn't tell me what you were doing, going through my things."

The words stung, even though Sydney told herself it was just his way. It didn't have to be his way. He chose it to be.

"I wasn't going through your things," she replied tersely. "I was looking for paper."

He wanted to believe her, but Barbara had taught him that relationships were filled with lies. "Big difference between photographs and paper."

She knew what he was saying. That she should have just left the photographs alone when she'd seen them.

"I got curious," she admitted. Wasn't he human? Didn't he ever get curious about anything? About anyone? "I figured I wasn't intruding on national security, or your secret identity, so I looked."

Sara stopped playing. Her mouth fell open. "You have a secret identity?"

Shayne slanted an annoyed look at Sydney. Trust her to fuel a misunderstanding. "No, I—"

Mac had walked in on his sister's question. He was clearly impressed. "Like Batman?"

"No, not like Batman," Shayne denied patiently. "And I don't have a secret identity. That's just Sydney talking." Sydney, he thought, was always talking.

Making use of the diversion, Sydney got up and indicated a corner of the room. "I thought you could put the tree there."

Maybe solitude had gotten the better of him, relegating his mind into a slower mode. Whatever the reason, he was having a really difficult time keeping up with her. As usual, he had no idea what she was talking about.

He followed her over to the corner. "What tree?"

Sara was quick to join them. "The Christmas tree, Daddy," she informed him. Sara gave him a pitying look, as if he'd just taken his first giant step into senility.

That, too, he figured, was Sydney's fault.

Most everything these days was Sydney's fault.

Sydney saw the look on his face and retreated a little. All right, so he didn't like her redecorating his house. She could understand that.

"Maybe I'm taking too much on myself..." she began.

He didn't let her finish. Instead, he stared at her incredulously. "Maybe?" How could she possibly think otherwise? With every breath she took, she pushed further and further into his life, changing things, disorienting him.

She did not take offense at his tone. "Okay, where do you usually put the tree?"

"I don't put it anywhere. I don't have a tree in the house." It wasn't until the words were out of his mouth that he realized how scroogelike that had to sound to his children.

Sara stared at him in alarm. "Doesn't Christmas come here?"

Mac gave her a disgusted big brother look. Didn't she know anything? "Sure it does. Christmas comes everywhere." He stole a glance at Sydney for confirmation. "Doesn't it?"

"That it does," she agreed quickly before Shayne could say anything else to make things worse. "And to prove it, your dad's going to put up the prettiest tree you ever saw. Right, 'Dad'?" Sydney looked at him expectantly.

It felt really strange, hearing her address him that way. As if they were a family. Which they weren't. And couldn't be.

When he looked at his children, two sets of eyes were staring back at him with expectations and hopes he couldn't bring himself to dash.

"Right," he agreed as he took Sydney's arm. "Could I have a word with you?"

"Always." With a fluid movement, she disengaged herself from him. "But it's going to have to wait until I get a couple of kids off to bed." It was late and past their bedtime. She looked at Sara and Mac, a warm, coaxing smile on her lips. "Right?"

Neither child looked very happy about the prospect of going off to bed Sydney thought, but they both reluctantly agreed and chorused a halfhearted, "Right." Both seemed to know that it was far too close to Christmas to put up any sort of a real fuss.

With his chess piece in check on the board, Shayne had no choice but to wait until after his children were asleep before he could talk to Sydney. Maybe it was better that way. It'd give him time to pull his thoughts about her together.

As if there was that much time in the world.

"All right, you can yell at me now."

Coming into his room, Sydney eased the door closed behind her. She didn't want him waking up the children after she'd spent so much effort getting them to sleep.

Surprised, Shayne looked up from the book he was reading. Unable to collect his thoughts, he'd felt it appropriate to peruse the pages of Shakespeare's *Taming of the Shrew*. After a while, he'd given up waiting for her to get back to him and just lost himself in the play.

He'd gained very little insight, but at least he'd been entertained.

Shayne sat up on the bed, swinging his legs over the side. The thick green cover joined the gold-edged pages, losing his place for him. "What makes you think I'm going to yell at you?"

He probably resented the image. "All right, not yell. Speak sternly," she amended, crossing to him. "Isn't that what you intended to do earlier? Put me in my place?"

He was no longer sure what he'd intended earlier. She could make him lose his train of thought faster than anything he'd ever known. "Maybe I would, if I knew where that was."

She looked down at him uncertainly. "Meaning?"

She would ask him to explain. "Meaning I know where I should put you, but I don't know if I want to put you there. And even if I wanted to, I don't know if I could." She was grinning broadly at him. He stopped talking. "What?"

"Don't look now, but you're beginning to sound like me." She thought it was adorable.

He sighed, dragging his hand through his hair. "Oh, God, it's worse than I thought."

"Is it?" Her grin melted into a soft smile. "Define 'worse.'"

That wasn't going to be easy, not where she was concerned. He rose from the bed to face her. "Look, after Barbara left, I finally made peace with the way my life was going to be."

Sydney doubted if peace was the word he was looking for. It was more as if he'd withdrawn from life altogether. But she let him talk. "And that was?"

"Solitary."

If that were true, he would have abandoned his practice and become a hermit. "Makes being a doctor difficult."

Shayne was determined to prove her wrong, at least about something. "Not really. You minister to their bodies and go on."

That's not the kind of doctor he was, no matter what he wanted to believe. She'd seen him with patients. Parts of him, of his compassion, came through in their care, no matter what he was trying to convince himself of.

"You're talking about assembling cars on a conveyor belt. People need more than that. People need to be comforted, to know that they're cared about as well as cared for." She saw that he was about to disagree, and retreated. It was enough that she'd made her point. "But I digress. You were talking about your life's plan. Go on."

For two cents, Shayne would wipe that smug look off her face. For less than that...

He felt himself getting stirred again. He tried to ignore the effect she had on him.

"Yeah, well, the plan I'd settled on was being alone. Then Barbara died and I got my kids back. Kids I didn't know what to do with."

Didn't he realize that he'd gone beyond that stage? "You're doing all right now."

He looked at her. Shayne was very aware of the debt he owed her. She'd been the one who'd turned Sara around. And Mac after that. Without her, who knew how long it would have taken them to come about, if at all?

"That was your doing."

"Not really." She didn't want him to minimize his effect on the children. They loved him very much. "Sometimes you need a catalyst, that's all. I got elected."

A catalyst. What a strange way to think of herself. Had she affected everything around her—his life—without being affected herself? Was that what she was telling him? Damn, when did life get so complicated?

He knew when. The moment she'd stepped off the plane and into his life. "That's just my problem. I don't know what to make of my catalyst."

The smile on her lips curled right through him, going from his gut straight to his toes.

"Maybe you don't have to make something of her." She moved closer to him. Or was that him, moving toward her? He wasn't clear on that. Wasn't clear on very much, except that he wanted her. "Maybe you just have to let her be. As in exist, not as in alone," she clarified, lest he misunderstand.

He seized the word. "It'd be best if I could leave *her* alone." He threaded his arms around her waist, pulling her to him. Feeling the heat begin to flare. "But I don't think I can."

She settled against him. "Are you coming on to me, Doctor?"

He wasn't sure he knew how to come on to a woman. That was something he'd never taken the time to pick up from Ben. "Clumsily."

Is that what he thought? Her eyes on his, Sydney moved her head from side to side. "You underestimate yourself, Shayne. There isn't a single clumsy thing about you."

Then why did he feel like a clumsy adolescent instead of a skilled physician who'd done more than his share of intricate surgery?

His hands were steady, his nerves were not. Shayne slowly began coaxing the first button of her blouse from its hole with the tips of his fingers when he stopped and looked toward the door.

She read his mind. "They're sound asleep." But, she knew, children were known to wake up at the worst possible moments. "And you have a lock."

It was better to be safe than sorry. Shayne crossed to the door and flipped the lock into place, then returned to her. She could think clearly when he couldn't. "You're always one step ahead of me."

She sincerely doubted it. Right now, she just wanted to be in sync with him. "I'll try to watch that," she promised softly.

His fingers occupied with the next button, Shayne pressed a kiss to her throat, sending the pulse there throbbing. He smiled to himself. "I'd appreciate it."

With his every touch, desire skittered along her body like tiny fireflies released from their prison and escaping toward freedom. He made her skin tingle and her pulse throb. Most of all, he made her want. Want with every fiber of her being that wondrous feeling that only came when he kissed her.

She shivered as he slowly removed the blouse from her shoulders, felt her loins tightening as the sleeves slid from her arms. The blouse fell to the floor as he toyed with the button on her jeans.

Heart pounding, she found his mouth and lost herself in his kiss.

Her moan served only to send Shayne over the brink that he'd been tottering on so precariously. He knew there was no use trying to hang on to his common sense; this time, he didn't waste the effort in trying. It was far more pleasurable using that energy in other ways.

In making love with her.

He hurried her out of the remainder of her clothes, his breath catching as she did the same. Each eager to find their way into the paradise they'd unwittingly stumbled into before.

Possessively, he skimmed his hands along her body, over and over again, until he could have recreated every curve, every nuance, that was Sydney with his eyes closed.

It wasn't enough.

He wanted more.

A starving man, he'd taken a morsel and found himself hopelessly craving more. Even if it meant his undoing.

Tumbling onto his bed, they feasted on one another, exploring not only each other's bodies, but the sensations that being together created. Sensations that were not entirely grounded in the physical act of lovemaking but in the feelings created by the act itself.

Lips sealed to hers, Shayne rolled over to gather her

closer to him. He caught his breath as a fresh, different heat flared from his side, rivaling the flame that was consuming him.

She felt his gasp play along her lips and pulled back, searching his face. He looked paler, stunned. "What's the matter?"

The pain he'd felt had settled down, the way it had all the other times in the past few days. Shayne dismissed it instantly. His body looming over hers, he framed her face with his hands.

"The matter is—" he grazed her mouth, once, twice and again "—you talk too much."

He was obliterating her thoughts. She struggled to protest. "But—'

He wouldn't let her get the words out. He didn't want to discuss the strange pain that intermittently brandished his side like a hot sword.

Right now, all he wanted to do was make love with her. Everything else could be dealt with later. Much, much later.

Shayne kissed her protest away. Kissed away everything but the need she had to feel his body joined with hers.

Shayne made love to her with every part of his body. He melted her with his kisses, inflamed her with his caresses, and drove her to the edge of madness with hands that were far more skilled than any surgeon's.

He made love with her as if he were on fire. When she could still think, she wondered what had come over him, but the speed, the tempo, the mood he'd struck fed her own desire, her own passions. She forgot about the promises she'd made to herself in the wee hours of the night, when disappointment loomed large and happiness was something that seemed light-years removed.

Forgot everything but Shayne.

He was making her crazy and she knew that she had to have him, had to feel his hands on her body, his lips skimming lightly, teasingly, maddeningly over every part of her.

She was light and air, sea and sun. She was all things wondrous and pure, and he felt almost humbled with the gift she was giving him. Had he had just a little of his mind, he would have said the burden of that gift was far too great for him to bear. But those were the feelings of a thinking man, a man who'd loved and lost and sworn never to be hurt again.

He had no thoughts, only desires that gave him no peace with their demands. He had to have her, for she was his salvation. She was the light at the end of the lonely tunnel he'd been traveling in all these long, solitary years.

He wanted to tell her, wanted her to know what she meant to him, what she did for him. The words burned in his throat, on his lips, but somehow he couldn't release them. Even now, in the midst of the madness that seized him, something held him back.

So instead, he lost himself in the passion, in the throes of desire, and gave her a night that he prayed would be burned into her very soul.

Eyes on hers, he sheathed himself within her, feeling her breath on his face as she gasped his name. He laced his fingers with hers and began to move his hips slowly, then more and more intensely. He meant to watch her, meant to see her reaction as rapture came to claim them both. Meant to. But the feeling swept him up, as well.

Shayne could only hang on as it swallowed him up and took him for its own.

Chapter Fifteen

Sydney knew the moment Shayne withdrew from her. Even before he physically moved aside. Knew by the emptiness, chilling and distant, that encroached over her, seizing her in its grip.

She wanted to reach for him, to assure herself she was wrong, to banish the feeling from her that was so awful. Pride kept her still.

What was he thinking? Shayne upbraided himself. He wasn't Ben. He was supposed to keep a tight rein over his feelings, his yearnings.

Supposed to.

He rolled onto his back and stared at the ceiling. Wishing he didn't want her as much as he did. Wishing that having her didn't breed a desire to have her again and again. He knew what happened when he allowed himself to become dependent on someone.

Stoically, he stared ahead of him, resisting the desire

to slip his arm around her. To hold her and tell himself that this time, it would be different. This time, he'd found someone who would stay. How could she, when it was his brother she'd been attracted to? Ben, with his quick wit and his joy of life. Ben was all airy clouds and dreams. Shayne was the rocky ground below.

"We shouldn't have done that."

His words cut across her heart like a scalpel. "We, or you?"

He didn't want to get into an argument about it and seized the one excuse she could appreciate. "The children wouldn't understand."

She could feel tears stinging her eyes. It was small to hide behind defenseless children. "The children are asleep."

Unable to lay by her side like this and not take her into his arms, no matter what he was trying to convince himself of, Shayne sat up. The vague pain was back, distracting him, adding to his load. Frustrated, he ran his hands through his hair.

"They wake up, they go looking. You know that." He had to struggle to keep from snapping at her. Didn't she realize what he was going through? "I'm not up to explaining it to either of them."

The chill around her rivaled the cold outside. Sydney drew herself up, holding the sheet to her. "How about yourself? Are you up to explaining it to yourself?"

There was something in her tone that made him turn to look at her. "What?"

"Never mind." Angry, hurt, all she wanted to do was get out of the room and away from him before she broke down. In a frenzied daze, she picked up her clothes and quickly pulled them on. She must have been crazy, falling in love with him. He didn't even want her. "Let me just go."

But he wasn't about to let her charge out of the room, not without explaining her comment. "What did you mean?" he demanded.

He knew damn well what she meant, Sydney fumed. Why was he trying to make this seem as if it were her fault? Still hurrying into her clothes, she glared at him.

"I mean, when you're making love with me, you're one person. But as soon as the moment is over, you change. You become afraid of what you feel. Afraid that it'll blow up on you just like the last time." She shoved her arms through her sleeves and fastened the buttons quickly, hoping he wouldn't notice that her hands were trembling. "Well, I have news for you. You're not alone in that lifeboat you're bobbing around in."

If she cried now, she was never going to forgive herself. Closing the snap on her jeans, she tossed her head. "Some of us in this relationship have the very same feelings and fears. Some of us have been cast adrift not once, but twice, and it's damn scary for us, too."

Regret began to weave its way through his confusion. "Sydney—"

Barefoot, holding her shoes in her hand, she was at the door. "I'm going to my room." Sydney flipped the lock and opened the door. "You stay nice and safe on your side of the world," she snapped as she stepped onto the hall. "Let me know if your boat springs a leak."

She shut the door behind her—not nearly as loud as she wanted to.

The night seemed endless. Sydney tossed and turned until she was sure she'd worn a hole in the mattress.

Sleep refused to relieve her. She wrestled with her thoughts, her feelings, for hours.

When morning arrived, leaving the sun to find its own way, Sydney had made up her mind. She couldn't take interacting with Shayne, knowing that he regretted making love with her. Maybe in time she could face him, but not right now. It hurt too much. She was going to move out. The cabin was nearly ready. They'd promised to have electricity restored by the end of the week.

As for the car, maybe it was foolish, but she wasn't going to wait for it to arrive. Ike had kiddingly told her that he'd be at her beck and call if she ever needed anything. She'd just have to take him up on that. Right after breakfast, she'd call Ike to see if he could help her move the rest of her things into the cabin. Especially the piano. If she had her piano with her, it wouldn't seem so lonely at night.

Or so she hoped.

And as for supplies, Sydney was certain she could prevail on Mr. Kellogg's son to bring them out to her. Someone would always be around to help. The rest of the citizens of Hades were a great deal friendlier toward her than Shayne was.

She intended to stop working at that clinic, too. He'd probably be a lot happier about that. There had to be something else she could do. Maybe she'd see about getting a teaching position, something she was more suited to doing. Anything so she didn't have to be near Shayne.

Boy, she thought, pulling on her boots, she could sure pick them. But this was it—really it. From now on, she was going to keep a firm lock on her heart. She wasn't going to love anything over the age of ten unless it had fur on it.

Her resolve in place, and determined to get things moving as quickly as possible, Sydney left her room. But as she passed Shayne's door, something—some tiny grain of residual affection—halted her in her tracks.

Stupid, stupid, stupid.

Calling herself names didn't seem to do any good. She couldn't get her feet to move.

So she knocked on his door, wanting to tell him she was going to be leaving. Wanting Shayne to tell her not to.

God, but she was an idiot.

There was no response to her knock. Listening at the door, she thought she heard him stirring. So now what? He was giving her the silent treatment, as well?

"Shayne?" No response. She knocked again, harder this time. Still nothing. If she'd had any brains, she'd just walk away, Sydney told herself.

Maybe she didn't have brains, but what she did have was a great deal of hurt pride. And anger. Wanting to vent at least the latter, she abandoned all niceties and opened the door.

Shayne was sitting up in bed, his hands on either side of him, gripping the mattress. His knuckles were white and there was a sheen of perspiration on his forehead. He looked like a man trying to summon the strength to stand up.

Something was very wrong. Sydney took a step across the threshold, looking at him uncertainly. "Shayne?"

He didn't answer. Instead, he raised his head and looked at her as if, until this moment, he hadn't realized she was in the room.

Newly formed plans crumbled instantly. Sydney crossed to the bed and looked at him more closely, almost afraid of what she'd see. There wasn't just a sheen of perspiration on his forehead, he was drenched.

Sydney dropped to her knees, feathering her hand across his forehead. It was hot. "What's the matter? Are you sick?"

Shayne shook his head, gritting his teeth. He pressed his fingers against his side, trying to press the pain away. It was the only way he could answer her. There were swords running through his side. "Just waiting for the pain to go away."

"Pain?" She looked him up and down quickly, as if pain had left a visible calling card. "What pain?" And then she noticed the way he was holding his right side. A single word came to mind. "Describe it to me."

Why couldn't she just go away and leave him in peace? Shayne groaned. He didn't need anyone badgering him right now. He hadn't the strength for it. Served him right for saying anything at all.

"I'm the doctor. I don't need to describe my pain to you."

Just because he was a doctor didn't mean he couldn't get sick. Only that he was too stubborn to admit it. Refusing to be intimidated by his attitude, she lightly pressed his side. His sharp intake of breath told her all she wanted to know.

"No, you need to admit you have appendicitis. Acute appendicitis from the looks of it."

It would pass. The pain had passed before. "I don't—"

She wasn't about to let him offer any feeble excuses or try to bully her away. Compassion mixed with her determination to help him, even if the man didn't want to be helped.

"I had it myself when I was sixteen. My cousin had

it at summer camp when she was twelve. I know the signs.'' She thought back to when they'd made love, and the way he'd winced for no apparent cause. ''This has been going on for a while now, hasn't it?''

It took effort to draw a breath. Shayne tried to think past the pain. He wasn't having a great deal of luck. ''Yes. Happy?''

She wished he was all right so she could slug him. ''What would make me happy is if you stopped being so damn stubborn and let me help you.''

He glared at her. It was hard to do when his eyelids insisted on drooping. Shayne fought to remain focused and not give in to the pain.

''Me stubborn? You're the most damn stubborn human being I've ever met.'' He tried to move her aside, but she stepped back, out of reach. Shayne found himself moving only air. ''Now if you'd give me a little privacy, I'd like to get dressed.'' A fresh wave of pain came, making gooseflesh out of the skin on his arms. He knew she noticed. There was no use in fighting this. She was right. ''All right, I'll stop being stubborn, as you put it, and fly myself to Anchorage.''

'''Anchorage'?'' she echoed.

''It's the nearest hospital—'' And he, he knew, was going to need surgery.

Before he could finish his sentence, Sydney had already gathered the clothes he'd left on the floor. She dumped them beside him on the bed. ''Stay right there, I'll dress you.''

''I—''

What he wanted to say was that he could dress himself. But he couldn't. He couldn't even argue with her about it. He was too weak and getting weaker by the minute. So he sat on the edge of the bed, feeling like a helpless child as Sydney quickly pulled a shirt over him, then coaxed his jeans over each leg.

"You can't fly that plane in your condition," she informed him tersely, her heart beating fast. Shayne looked awful, she thought. "I'm going to take you to Anchorage."

He was vaguely aware that she was pulling on his boots. "We can't drive there this time of year." The roads were impassable.

"I know." Even if they could, the trip would take too long and she wasn't sure just how long he had. She rose to her feet. "We'll go by plane."

Shayne stared at her. Was she saying what he thought she was saying? "You're going to fly?" Maybe he was hallucinating, after all.

Sydney did her best to look confident. "You're going to talk me through it."

He snorted, shaking his head. "The hell I am."

Sydney fixed him with the same look she'd give any third grader who acted up in her class.

"You have a choice. You either talk me through the flight, or talk me through your surgery, your choice. Because it's for damn sure that's not about to go away this time—" she nodded at his throbbing side "—and you're in no condition to fly on your own." Taking his arm, she helped him to his feet, then positioned herself so that she could place his arm over her shoulder. "Now lean on me so that we can get down the stairs in something under two hours."

Shayne did as she ordered. Every step hurt and felt as if he were taking it on legs that had been constructed out of gelatin. He could feel her struggling under his weight and hated the fact that he couldn't move on his own power. "Aren't you going to carry me fireman-style?"

"Very funny." She got a better grip on his arm, wishing his bedroom had been downstairs. At least then she wouldn't have so far to walk. "Next time."

By the time they made it down the stairs, Sydney's legs were beginning to feel like rubber. She made it to the sofa, then eased him down as gently as she could.

"Stay here for a minute," she said, sucking air into her aching lungs. "I've got to make a phone call"

He wanted to protest, to say he was going to fly himself and that was that. All he could do was sink onto the sofa.

Their passage hadn't gone unnoticed. Awakened by the noise, Mac and Sara had each ventured out of their rooms, curious. Mac was the first one down the stairs. He looked at his father, afraid of what he saw.

Mac turned to Sydney. "Is Dad all right?"

Sydney glanced at the boy, hoping she looked and sounded more confident than she felt. "He's going to be fine, honey." Quickly, she pressed the numbers on the telephone keypad, hoping that Ike was home and answering his phone.

Standing behind Mac, Sara began to cry. "He's going to die, like Mama."

Shayne reached for Sara, hardly having enough strength to stretch out his arm. She huddled against him. "I'm not going to die, Sara."

"Not if I have anything to say about it," Sydney promised all of them. She just prayed it wasn't an empty promise. And then, hearing the receiver being picked up, her attention was riveted to the man on the other end.

"Ike, it's Sydney."

"How's Alaska's most beautiful woman?"

"Desperate." She hurried on before he could comment. "Listen carefully, Ike. I need you to come here and stay with the children." Asia wouldn't be coming until later, and Sydney had no way to reach her since the woman didn't have a phone. She needed someone here now. "I've got to get Shayne to the hospital at Anchorage." Because she saw fear in the children's eyes, she reworded what she was about to say. "I think his appendix is on the verge of going."

"Anchorage?" Ike sounded doubtful. "Is he up to flying the plane?"

She glanced at Shayne. He didn't look up to even walking. "No, I'm taking him."

"You're flying?" Ike asked, incredulous.

Sydney licked her lips. Was it too early to start praying? "I'm going to try."

"Darlin', you'd better do more than try." Ike thought a minute. "I'll call Tate and see if his son—no, damn, he said the kid was going to be gone until tomorrow." There was no one else to fly a plane. He fervently hoped her flying lessons had stuck. "I'll be right there."

She looked at Shayne. They were going to need every minute they could find. "I've got to leave with him now, Ike. Hurry. The kids are going to be alone until you get here."

"Already gone— And Sydney…"

She'd almost hung up. Quickly, she pressed the receiver to her ear again. "Yes?"

"Good luck."

She laughed, but there was no humor in the sound. "Thanks." She knew she was going to need it. By the bucketful.

Shayne was beginning to feel strange, light-headed. As if he were winking in and out of his head. How could he talk her through anything? "Sydney, we could get a dogsled—"

She could just picture that. Sydney hurried to get their parkas. "Right, and when the snow melts in the spring, they can find us huddled together." Quickly, carefully, she slipped his parka on Shayne, then shrugged into her own. "Flying's our only option." She gave him the best confident grin she could muster. "What's the matter, don't you trust yourself as a teacher?"

His teaching abilities had nothing to do with it. "You've never gone up."

And wasn't she acutely aware of that? Sydney shrugged cavalierly.

"Always a first time." She just prayed it wouldn't be her last. She was already at the front door. Her heart ached at the expression on the children's face. "I'll taxi the plane as close to the house as I can, then come and get you."

Adrenaline double-timing through every part of her body, she hurried out.

Somehow, with Mac doing his best to help, Sydney managed to get a much weakened Shayne into the cockpit. Hands trembling from the strain, she quickly secured his seat belt, then turned to look at the worried faces of the two children clustered around her.

Time was precious, but she shaved a little off to kneel between them. She placed a hand on either of their shoulders, making them a promise she knew they needed to hear.

"I'm not going to let anything happen to him, you hear? Nothing. Ike's coming to take care of you and I'll call as soon as I can. Mac, I want you to take your sister inside and take care of her until Ike gets here. Okay?"

He nodded, placing one arm around Sara's small shoulders. And then he looked at her with Shayne's eyes. "You promise you won't let anything happen to him?"

"I promise." She hugged them both quickly, then rose to her feet. It was all the time she could spare.

Sydney felt drenched as she climbed into the plane. Helping Shayne up to and then into the plane had been harder than she'd thought.

He turned his head and looked at her. She saw the uncertainty in his eyes.

"Don't worry, I'll get you there in one piece." She secured the door, trying not to shiver. Her clothes were sticking to her back. "And when you're on your feet again, you can treat me for pneumonia."

Lips dry as dust, Shayne struggled to hold on to consciousness. "Sydney—"

She didn't want him wasting his breath. "Save your strength. I'm going to need you to talk me through the rough patches."

Heart in her mouth, she turned the key, pumped gasoline through the lines, then pressed the button to engage the ignition. The engine came to life. As she began the short run to take off, Sydney could feel every pulse in her body throbbing.

Sometimes fear was a good thing, she told herself. Sometimes, it kept you alert.

Everything within her galvanized, Sydney concentrated on the controls, trying to remember everything Shayne had taught her.

The pain was getting unmanageable. Like some huge alien creature, it was sucking away his thoughts, leaving a void. It took him a moment, or maybe longer, to realize that there was nothing but sky around them. Perfect blue sky.

"We're airborne."

He sounded as surprised as she felt. First part down, lots more to go, she told herself, trying to hang on to the confidence the takeoff had generated.

She let out the breath she'd been holding. "Yes, and without our own personal set of wings, too." And, with just a little luck, she could keep it that way.

Smiling, she looked to her right. "How are you doing?" Not well, she could see that. Fear reared its head again, larger than before. She had to reach the hospital in time. She *had* to. "Are you all right, Shayne?"

He struggled to stay conscious. "As all right as I can be." Each word was an effort, but there were some he had to say. "Sydney, if anything happens to me—"

She didn't want to go there. "Nothing's going to happen." She was aware that the words strained through her teeth. "You hear me? You're going to be fine. I can land this thing."

Right, God? I can do this. Please, I'll never ask You for anything else again, just let me land this thing safely.

Shayne wasn't thinking about the landing. He knew she could do it, through sheer grit. But patients out here died before they received medical attention and he knew that he had waited too long.

"But if it does," he persisted. "I want you to take care of Sara and Mac."

"Don't worry about it." She didn't want him dwelling on the negative. He was going to be fine, just fine. She wasn't going to let him die. And then, because he needed to hear her promise, she said, "I will."

Shayne knew he could count on her. It was going to be all right. He could let go if he knew Sydney would be there for them. He should have put up more of a fight to have them in his life. And less of a fight to push Sydney out of it.

"And Sydney..."

"What?" She realized she'd snapped the word. Her hands were rigid on the wheel. "Sorry, just a little edgy. What do you want to tell me?"

"I love you."

Only extreme concentration kept Sydney from dipping the plane. "You really have to work on your timing, Shayne." He was delirious, she thought. He probably wouldn't even remember saying that to her once this was over. "Hang on, we're almost there." When he didn't say anything, she glanced at him. He was slumped in his seat, his eyes shut. Her heart stopped. "Shayne? Oh, God." Flipping on the autopilot switch, she felt his chest. It was moving. He was alive.

Sydney reclaimed control of the plane, then fumbled for the radio. "Anchorage, I'm a small Cessna heading your way and I have a very big problem. Do you read me?"

After what felt like an eternity, she heard a crackling noise.

"Cessna, this is Anchorage. We read you loud and clear. What's your problem?"

The sound of another voice, a calm, competent resonant male voice, almost made her cry.

"I'm flying Dr. Shayne Kerrigan to the hospital. He has acute appendicitis and he's just passed out." It was going to be all right, she told herself. It was. Never mind that her whole body felt as if a squadron of ants was moving up and down it. "And, Anchorage... I've never flown before. Talk me down, please."

"Cessna, this is going to be smooth as silk," the voice promised.

She blinked back tears. "I'm going to hold you to that."

Her bones only turned to liquid afterward, as she stood in the hospital waiting area after what seemed like a thousand years later. The landing had been bumpy, but they'd made it. There was a medical helicopter waiting for them and she and Shayne had been whisked off to the hospital. She'd held Shayne's hand all the way there. He'd never regained consciousness.

She'd lived in terror for the entire two hours that the surgery had taken. Twice as long, she knew, as it should have. But that was because, she was told later, Shayne's appendix had burst on the operating table, making the surgery that much more complicated.

She'd kissed the surgeon when he'd come out of the operating room to tell her that Shayne was going to be all right.

Now, feeling oddly disembodied, she hit the numbers to Shayne's home. The phone was picked up on the first ring. She heard Ike's voice.

"Hello, Ike? It's Sydney."

"Thank God. You made it then." He didn't begin to tell her the thoughts that had been going through his head as he'd tried to distract Shayne's children from the drama happening beyond their reach.

"No, they've installed phones in heaven." She laughed giddily, so grateful the ordeal was over. So grateful she'd made it just in time. "Yes, we made it. They just finished operating on him. Doctor says he's going to be all right." She'd never let herself believe anything else. But now that it was over, now that she had said the words out loud, she realized how terrified she'd been. "Give me the kids, will you? Hold the receiver between them."

"Sure thing. They're right here, tugging on me."

She heard the sound of the receiver being moved. The next thing she knew, she heard both children shouting her name.

"Sydney, is he...?" Mac's voice trailed off.

"You dad's going to be fine, Mac. The doctor just came out and told me so."

"When can Daddy come home?" Sara wanted to know.

"In about three or four days." Sooner if he had anything to say about it, if she knew him. "I'll be home as soon as I can and tell you all about it."

She heard the receiver being transferred again and then Ike was on the line. "Hey, Earhart, why don't you stay there awhile until you're in shape to fly again? I can take care of the kids."

She wanted to get back, to reassure the children in person. Shayne would be asleep for most of the rest of the day. "I'm fine, Ike."

"You bet you are." He laughed.

As if she were handling something very fragile, Sydney carefully replaced the telephone receiver into its cradle. Then, with her back against the wall, she slid bonelessly to the floor and covered her face with both hands as relief flooded through her.

He was going to be all right.

Chapter Sixteen

Stepping away from the small Twin Otter, Sydney waved at Jeb Kellogg as he initiated takeoff. He'd just refused her invitation to come in for a cup of coffee and some pie. There was a load of fresh produce and dairy products waiting to be delivered to his father's store. The round trip to Anchorage to pick Shayne up from the hospital had taken longer than they had anticipated.

But that was because Shayne's doctor hadn't really wanted to release him. He'd wanted Shayne to remain one more day. Shayne had been very vocal about his thoughts on that matter.

Sydney had thought he should remain, too. But her opinion obviously counted for less than the doctor's, if Shayne's tone was any indication. Still, she wished he'd given in and agreed to stay the extra day. He looked thinner. It was the first thing that she really noticed coming into the hospital this morning, that he was thinner.

Not thin, just thinner. Four days had made a difference and he'd been through a lot, including peritonitis.

Shayne had waved it off, claiming the hospital food was responsible for his weight loss.

Knowing she wouldn't get anywhere arguing with him, Sydney had dropped the subject.

"C'mon, let's get you inside," Ike said, slinging Shayne's arm over his shoulder. They were almost the same height. The arrangement made for awkward progress at best.

Thinner or not, it was wonderful to see Shayne again, Sydney thought. She'd stayed away those four days, calling the hospital to see how he was doing. Sydney figured he needed the time away from her, and besides, she had Sara and Mac to care for, and the clinic to run. She'd rescheduled the patients with minor problems and rerouted the ones needing immediate attention to Anchorage. Jeb Kellogg had flown them there and back.

Leading the way into the house, Sydney looked over her shoulder at Shayne. "The nurses told me you were the worst patient they'd had in quite a while."

"Sounds about right," Ike agreed.

Shayne couldn't argue with the evaluation. "Occupational habit when you're a doctor. You don't like having anyone around, telling you they know what's best for you."

And that would be her, she thought. He was giving her a not-so-subtle message about their relationship. "So let me get this straight, that's why you became a doctor, to fit your personality? Because you wouldn't have liked anyone telling you they knew better than you even if you were a kayak salesman?"

God, but it was good to see her. All the way over from Anchorage, all Shayne could do was look at her. And realize over and over again how much he'd missed seeing her. "You could be right."

Sydney's hands flew to her chest, covering one another. "Wait, my heart. I don't think I can stand the strain of the all-knowing Shayne Kerrigan admitting someone else was right besides him."

She hadn't changed any. His mouth curved. "You saved my life, I'll let that pass."

Sydney turned from the front door. "I saved your life and you'll let a lot of things pass."

He exchanged looks with Ike. "Why do I get the feeling she'll hold me to that?"

"Because I will," she answered simply. Before opening the door, she stopped. He could do with a bit of coaching. "Now there are two small children in there who have lived in terror of your not coming back. I want you to give them the biggest, most reassuring grin you can muster."

Ike laughed. "Hell, then they won't know it's Shayne."

Shayne was growing impatient as well as weary. He hated feeling weak, it left him far too vulnerable. "You don't have to tell me how to behave with my kids."

She wasn't about to back down, not when it came to Sara and Mac. They were too impressionable. "Someone has to. Might as well be me. Ready?"

The sigh was more of a huff. "Just open the door, Sydney."

"Do as he says, darlin'," Ike begged. "This man's no featherweight."

The moment she opened the front door, Sara and Mac poured out onto the porch as if they'd been hovering behind the door all afternoon. Between them, they almost managed to knock Shayne down. If Ike hadn't been supporting him, they probably would have.

Sara buried her face in the bottom of his parka, her small arms unable to reach around him for the bear hug she so desperately wanted to give him. "Daddy, you're back."

He laid his hand on her head, stroking it. "I said I would be."

She raised her head to look up at him. "We thought…"

He knew what she thought. What he'd thought, too. There was no purpose in going there. "Never mind that now, I'm all right."

Mac grinned, looking at Sydney. "Just like Sydney said."

"Yes, just like Sydney said," Shayne agreed.

"And now Sydney says, everybody get inside before you all get sick." Sydney shooed them all into the house. "I'm not about to play Nancy Nurse to the lot of you."

With a child on either side of him, Shayne entered the house he'd lived in all of his life. And thought how wonderful it was to be home again.

Sydney'd been busy in his absence, he noted. There was what looked to be at least a nine-foot tree standing in the corner, decked out in decorations he didn't recognize.

"See you put up a tree."

She couldn't tell by his tone if he was annoyed at her presumption. That much hadn't changed about him, he still left her guessing. "Had to do something to keep them occupied."

Sara ran over to the sofa and hurried back with a small, rectangular box. Silver streamers protruded out of an opening, catching the light and gleaming. Sara offered the box to her father. "We saved the tinsel for you."

Sydney laid a restraining had on Sara's shoulder. "Your dad's not up to throwing tinsel yet, Sara. Maybe tomorrow."

But Shayne wanted to join in, to experience every-thing as if he'd been given a second chance to make up for all his shortcomings and all the time he'd lost.

"Sure I am." Gingerly, he picked several strands from the box and pitched them toward the tree. They fell almost a foot short.

"And that, ladies and gentlemen," Sydney murmured glibly, "is one of the main reasons why Alaska has no official baseball team. No local talent."

Mac quickly scrambled to pick up the strands, gloss-ing over his father's failure.

"That's okay, Dad, you can do this later." He de-posited the tinsel on the coffee table. "Christmas is still a couple of days off."

Christmas. The word finally sank in. Christmas was almost here and he had nothing to give either of them. He'd put off shopping and now it was too late.

"Might be longer than that," Shayne commented un-der his breath. How did he go about telling them that he didn't have anything for them? What kind of a father did that make him?

"Don't bet the clinic on it," Ike whispered in his ear. Shayne looked at him quizzically. Ike nodded toward Sydney who was hurrying up the stairs to get Shayne's bed ready. "She took care of things for you in that de-partment." He should know. He helped her carry the things she'd bought at the general store to the four-by-four. Ike looked at Shayne significantly. "I'd say she takes damn good care of you in every department." And then he shrugged carelessly. "But then, that'd be just me talking."

"Something you do an awful lot of," Shayne agreed.

He owed her a great deal, Shayne thought. More, he was beginning to believe, than he could ever hope to pay back.

Ike shifted, getting a better grip around Shayne's

waist. He turned toward the stairs. "And I'm going to do just a mite more talking while I get you up to your room. I don't have to tell you competition's stiff around here. You don't start acting like the smart man you are," he warned Shayne, "one fine day you're going to find yourself real empty-handed."

Shayne already knew that, but he'd just endured four days of poking and prodding. Not in the best of humors, he bristled at Ike's presumption. "Is that supposed to mean something to me?"

Ike stopped at the landing, getting a second wind. He turned toward Shayne's room.

"Yeah, it is." A few more steps and Ike deposited Shayne onto the bed. He'd had lighter loads to maneuver. "Okay, patient's all yours, darlin'. Not much to look at, but hell, we knew that already, didn't we?" He grinned, backing out of the room. "See you two around."

Sydney walked him just to the doorway. "Thanks for everything, Ike." And then she turned her attention to Shayne. He looked exhausted. Probably bite her head off if she mentioned it, though. "Anything I can get you?"

When he shook his head, it didn't surprise her. "No, you've already done plenty."

Sydney laughed softly to herself. "Well, that much hasn't changed. I still don't know if what you're saying is a compliment or a criticism."

"It's neither. It's gratitude."

Her surprise melted into something softer. "That would explain why I didn't recognize it. You've never offered it before."

There was so much he wanted to say to her, if he could only find the words. "Maybe I should have."

She smiled, seeing more in his eyes than she'd ever seen before. "Don't strain yourself your first time out."

Her smile widened. "I wouldn't want to have to fly you back to the hospital."

"I wouldn't want to have to go."

Again, she wasn't sure what he meant. Only what she wanted him to mean. "There's that quandary again." She moved toward the doorway. "I'll let you get some rest."

She was almost gone when she heard him call her name. "Sydney?"

Sydney ducked back inside the room. "Yes?"

"The tree looks nice."

She knew what it took for him to give out an actual compliment. Something a little shy of an act of Congress. She restrained the desire to fly back to his side and throw her arms around him. There was no way she could express how relieved she was that he was here, that he was alive.

"It'll look nicer with tinsel. Get your pitching arm in shape." And with that, she eased the door closed.

Shayne couldn't remember the last time Christmas had meant squeals, flying paper and joyous noise. Somewhere back in the early years of his childhood, probably. He sat on the sofa, absorbing it all. Thinking how much he enjoyed being in the center of this kind of chaos.

And he had Sidney to thank for it.

He had her to thank for a lot of things. Without Sydney, most of this wouldn't have happened. Hell, he probably wouldn't have been here to enjoy it, either. She'd given him back his life in more than one way.

"Wow, it's just what I wanted!" Mac cried. All smiles, he looked at Shayne as he clutched a box that contained the latest model of an electronic game system to his chest. "How did you know?"

There was a very simple explanation. He hadn't known. Hadn't been responsible for any of the myriad gifts that were scattered about, playing hide-and-seek with wrapping paper on his living room floor. It had all been Sydney's doing.

"Dads always know these kinds of things," Sydney told Mac, coming to Shayne's rescue.

She was always coming to his rescue, he thought, one way or another. She had from the very first.

"I just love my kitty," Sara said for the umpteenth time as she rubbed her face along the soft calico-colored fur.

"Be gentle with her," Sydney cautioned. "She's still a baby."

"I will," Sara promised solemnly.

Gingerly, Shayne stepped around the clutter to get to Sydney. It'd been two days since he'd come home and he was still feeling a little wobbly, but a great deal better than he had when he'd first walked through the door.

"Sydney, about what I said in the plane when you were taking me to the hospital…"

Wading through the sea of paper, she began picking it up. "You mean, when you asked me to take care of Sara and Mac if something—"

"No, after that."

Sydney turned away, picking up another flurry of paper, flattening it against the first pile. "You said something after that?"

With determination, he took the torn wrapping paper from her hands. She knew damn well he'd said something, something that desperation had prompted him to say. Something he meant. "I said I love you."

She looked at him, wondering what it was he wanted from her now. He'd already taken her heart and then walked over it. Wasn't that enough? What was this latest salvo he wanted to fire at her?

"You remember that?"

"Yes," he said quietly. This wasn't easy for him, but he owed it to her. Owed it to both of them.

She took a deep breath, shrugging off the feeling that was edging over her. "That's okay, I never hold a man to what he says just before he passes out. There's something in the Geneva convention about taking unfair advantage—"

Shayne knew what she was doing. She was throwing up a smoke screen. He wasn't about to let her. "What if the man wants to be held to it?" That, he saw, got her.

Sydney's mouth dropped open. "What?"

Before he could say anything more, Sara was tugging on her arm, pointing toward the tree behind her. "Sydney, there's a present for you."

She'd already opened up two boxes with handmade gifts from each of the children, gifts that warmed her heart. There'd even been a gift from Asia, gloves that the woman had made herself. There hadn't been one from Shayne, but then, realistically, she hadn't expected a gift. It was unrealistic that she'd cherished a tiny hope. Even she knew how foolish that was.

Sydney shook her head. Sara had to be mistaken. "I've already got my presents."

"No, there's one more," Mac insisted. "That little one right there." Both children were pointing toward the tree. Not under it but at the heart of it.

Confused, playing along, Sydney approached the Christmas tree. She didn't notice that Shayne was holding his breath, watching her every move.

And then she saw it. In the center of the profusely decorated Christmas tree was a tiny box suspended from a branch by a tiny, silver ribbon.

She could have sworn it wasn't there before.

Feeling suddenly very nervous, she plucked the box

from its perch. She took a deep breath. "Are you sure it's for me?"

Mac stood on his toes and looked over her arm. But he already knew what he was going to see. His dad had shown him the box before he'd hung it. Sharing the secret made him feel very important.

"Got your name on it," Mac told her.

She looked at it, then glanced up at Shayne. She would have known that handwriting anywhere. "So it does."

Damn, thought Shayne, even his palms felt sweaty. She did everything fast, why had she suddenly slowed her pace to that of frozen molasses? She was putting him through hell.

"You going to stand there with it all day, or are you going to open it?"

What she was doing was trying to quell her nervousness. "I like savoring things."

Then, as she began to slip off the ribbon, he suddenly looked at Sara and Mac. He needed this time alone with Sydney. Just in case.

"Kids, why don't you see if Asia has breakfast ready yet?"

"Okay." Sara, a miniature woman in the making, took Mac's hand and pulled him along behind her.

When Shayne looked back at Sydney, she was still holding the box in her hand. It was unopened.

Shayne took a breath. "Open it." Nerves danced all through him. He'd barely gotten the gift in time. He'd had to rely on Ike to select it and bring it to him. The complications had felt as if they were endless.

They'd all be worth it if she smiled.

Sydney could feel her hands shaking. They'd been steadier when she'd flown the plane to Anchorage. For some ridiculous reason, she was afraid that when she opened the gift, there wouldn't be anything there.

But there was. There was a black velvet box inside the paper. And ring inside of the box. A ring with a perfect small diamond mounted in the center of it.

Afraid to think, to let herself feel, she raised her eyes to his. "Shayne?"

He couldn't read her expression. Something twisted inside him. If she didn't want it, he didn't know what he was going to do.

Yes, he did. If he had to, he was going to beg her. This one time in his life, he'd humble himself and beg her to marry him. To stay in his life. Because he knew that life without her wasn't life at all.

"It's an engagement ring."

She wanted to laugh. She wanted to cry. "I know what it is. Why are you giving it to me?"

Was she rejecting him, after all? He took her hand. "Why do you think?"

That was just it, she couldn't think. Was afraid to think. "If this has anything to do with what you said to me in the plane, you don't have to feel obligated, Shayne. I—"

She was babbling. He placed a fingertip to her lips and stopped her words. "For once, will you please just let me talk?"

She pressed her lips together. "Sorry."

He hadn't meant to make that sound like an admonishment. This wasn't starting out right, he thought in frustration. Not knowing what else to do, he pushed on.

"I had a lot of time to think, lying awake in that hospital bed, listening to the intercom go off every few minutes." He was digressing. Because he was afraid of the outcome. "Time to think about how you were always coming to my rescue. I don't mean the plane flight—although I'd probably be dead by now if you hadn't gotten me there in time. I mean, in my life. Taking down the wall between Sara, Mac and me. Making me realize that I was only half a man if I couldn't feel things." Without realizing it, he took hold of her shoulders to wage the argument of his life. "You made me feel again, Sydney. You made me whole. Now make me happy, and say yes."

She was afraid to breathe, afraid that if she did, she'd wake up and find that all this was just a lovely dream. "You mean that?"

"I've never meant anything more in my life," Shayne swore.

Very slowly, she began to breathe. "And you're not going to disappear?"

"Where would I go?" He slipped his arms around her. "Everything I love is right here, in this house, in this room. In my arms."

Love. The word was so very precious to her. "You love me?"

"I love you." Once the words were out, he couldn't help wondering why they had been so hard to say. They seemed so easy now. "I've been afraid to say it, afraid to think it, but I do, Sydney. I really do, and I'll make you a good husband, I promise. If I don't, you can take me on another plane ride." He grinned, kissing her temple. "One I'll stay conscious for."

Her maiden run had been a bumpy one, but they had walked away alive and that was all that counted. "It's a deal."

Mouth stained with the remnants of the jelly doughnuts Sydney had stayed up late to make for them, Mac came running back into the room.

"What's a deal?" he asked around a mouthful of jelly.

Shayne looked down at his son's face. How did one man deserve to have this much happiness? "You're getting a new mom."

Confused, Mac frowned. "I don't want a new mom. I want Sydney."

The boy had good taste, Shayne thought. "You're in luck. Two birds with one stone."

Sara came running into the room, chasing her new kitten. Catching it, she stared at her father. "We're getting a bird?" In her excitement, she squeezed the kitten, who mewed a protest and wriggled in her arms.

"No, I think Taffy would have something to say about that." Shayne scratched the kitten's head. "But you are getting a new mom."

Sara took the news in stride. "Can I pick her out?" She didn't wait for an answer. "Because if I can, I pick Sydney."

Apparently his kids were way ahead of him here. "Then I guess it's unanimous."

Sara scowled, trying to understand the new word. "What's u-nanny-mouse?"

"It means that we're all going to be happy." Shayne looked at Sydney. "Right?"

Sydney put her arms around his neck. "You bet 'right.'"

"Are you two going to kiss now, or do you need mistletoe?" Mac looked around the room, just in case.

"We don't need excuses anymore." Sydney smiled up into Shayne's face. "Do we?"

"Nope."

And to prove it, he kissed her.

* * * * *

▼™ SILHOUETTE
SPECIAL EDITION®

AVAILABLE FROM 24TH DECEMBER 1999

BABY LOVE Victoria Pade

That's My Baby!

Rugged Ry McDermot is in trouble; named legal guardian to an adorable toddler, he is out of his depth. Tallie Shanahan is the solution to his problem. But playing house with Tallie is proving more tempting than this sworn bachelor would like!

JUST THE THREE OF US Jennifer Mikels

As a businesswoman, Taylor Elmhurst is a success, but as a guardian she has a lot to learn. Help unexpectedly comes in the form of sexy Matt Duran. A natural with her nephew, his interest soon extends to Taylor…

A WEDDING FOR MAGGIE Allison Leigh

Daniel Clay left town rather than watch Maggie wed another. Now she's a widow, and one stolen night of passion leads to an unplanned pregnancy; so will *he* be marrying Maggie after all?

THE COWBOY AND HIS WAYWARD BRIDE
Sherryl Woods

And Baby Makes Three

Harlan Adams has just discovered he's a father and he's furious! His childhood sweetheart, Laurie Jensen, has secretly given birth to their daughter. Now this determined dad won't take no for an answer— starting with his proposal!

HOMETOWN GIRL Robin Lee Hatcher

Monica Fletcher had cut Daniel Rourke out of her life forever, never dreaming that one day their daughter would need him. But now Daniel is back and determined to be a part of both of their lives!

THE SECRET MILLIONAIRE Patricia Thayer

Jill Morgan has accepted that to Rick Covelli she was just a fling. But he's back, and he says he's changed. Money's no object, but can Jill be wooed, given that she has to think of her child?

AVAILABLE FROM 24TH DECEMBER 1999

SILHOUETTE®

Intrigue

Danger, deception and desire

RYAN'S RESCUE Karen Leabo
A COWBOY'S HONOUR Laura Gordon
JACKSON'S WOMAN Judi Lind
REDHAWK'S RETURN Aimée Thurlo

Desire

Provocative, sensual love stories

SHEIKH'S RANSOM Alexandra Sellers
A MATCH FOR MORGAN Marie Ferrarella
THE MILLIONAIRE AND THE PREGNANT PAUPER
Christie Ridgway
THE STARDUST COWBOY Anne McAllister
SECRET DAD Raye Morgan
THE SCANDALOUS HEIRESS Kathryn Taylor

Sensation

A thrilling mix of passion, adventure and drama

THE TOUGH GUY AND THE TODDLER
Diane Pershing
LIKE FATHER, LIKE DAUGHTER Margaret Watson
THE MIRACLE MAN Sharon Sala
ONCE MORE A FAMILY Paula Detmer Riggs

Sometimes bringing up baby can bring surprises —and showers of love! For the cutest and cuddliest heroes and heroines, choose the Special Edition™ book marked

That's my baby!

FREE
4 BOOKS
AND A SURPRISE GIFT!

We would like to take this opportunity to thank you for reading this Silhouette® book by offering you the chance to take FOUR more specially selected titles from the Special Edition™ series absolutely FREE! We're also making this offer to introduce you to the benefits of the Reader Service™—

- ★ FREE home delivery
- ★ FREE monthly Newsletter
- ★ FREE gifts and competitions
- ★ Exclusive Reader Service discounts
- ★ Books available before they're in the shops

Accepting these FREE books and gift places you under no obligation to buy; you may cancel at any time, even after receiving your free shipment. Simply complete your details below and return the entire page to the address below. **You don't even need a stamp!**

YES! Please send me 4 free Special Edition books and a surprise gift. I understand that unless you hear from me, I will receive 6 superb new titles every month for just £2.70 each, postage and packing free. I am under no obligation to purchase any books and may cancel my subscription at any time. The free books and gift will be mine to keep in any case.

E9EC

Ms/Mrs/Miss/Mr ....Initials.................................

BLOCK CAPITALS PLEASE

Surname...

Address..

....

....Postcode ....

Send this whole page to:
UK: FREEPOST CN81, Croydon, CR9 3WZ
EIRE: PO Box 4546, Kilcock, County Kildare (stamp required)

Offer valid in UK and Eire only and not available to current Reader Service subscribers to this series. We reserve the right to refuse an application and applicants must be aged 18 years or over. Only one application per household. Terms and prices subject to change without notice. Offer expires 30th June 2000. As a result of this application, you may receive further offers from Harlequin Mills & Boon Limited and other carefully selected companies. If you would prefer not to share in this opportunity please write to The Data Manager at the address above.

Silhouette is a registered trademark used under license.

Special Edition is being used as a trademark.